THE HANGING JUDGE OF SPLIT ROCK

CHASE MASON GUNSLINGER SERIES BOOK 1

BRUCE EVERETT

SUMMARY

An exciting new Western series for readers who like fast-moving stories of the Old West.

On the search for his father's killer, Chase Mason performs a kindness for a stranger, Owen Montgomery. At the next town he stops in, he's accused of killing Montgomery. Jailed by a corrupt sheriff, Chase must prove his innocence before Hanging Judge Henry G. Hathaway arrives. Judge Hathaway is not known for his fairness, and the deck is stacked against Chase.

Fighting a crooked sheriff in a town full of corruption, Chase finds an unlikely ally in Montgomery's daughter Maggie, who has been threatened by a stranger.

Chase can't stop himself from defending those who can't defend themselves, even if it puts his own life in danger. It will take more than bad guys, bullets and the hangman's rope to stop Chase from finding justice.

CHAPTER ONE

Chase Mason pressed his back against a worn boulder as he listened to the crackling of his campfire. He loved this time of the night, when the dark encompassed everything but the area around the flickering fire. He stretched out his tall frame and settled down on his bedroll, his head propped on his saddle. He breathed in the smells of his campsite: leather from the saddle, the dried sweat of his horse Rebel and the smoke from his fire all helped to put him at ease.

Content, he put his arms behind his head and glanced up at the stars hanging in the moonless sky, and couldn't think of a better way to spend the night. He was more at home out here than in some hotel or tavern, trying to sleep in a room too small as his legs dangled over the end of the bed. His face held a relaxed smile as he drifted off to sleep.

Chase woke refreshed and eager to start the day. He rekindled the fire, prepared the coffee pot and placed it over the blaze. He checked on Rebel, who was grazing on a patch of grass. “Don’t worry, boy, I’ll get you some real food soon enough. We don’t have much further to ride.” The horse stopped eating, looked at Chase, then continued munching the little grass that remained. Returning to the fire, Chase filled his tin cup with strong, black coffee. As he held it in both hands, he thought of why he’d started this journey.

His father, Ned, had been a Pinkerton detective, shot in the line of duty when Chase was 10 years old. The doctor who worked on him that day removed the bullet from Ned’s back, but couldn’t save him. Chase kept the slug secured with rawhide string around his neck. He vowed to show it to his father’s killer right before Chase shot him. His mother had died years earlier from an illness, and after his father’s murder, he’d been taken in by a prostitute living upstairs in the local saloon. Though Maria made her living on her back, she was an honest woman. He learned all he needed to know about people and trusting his gut when things didn't seem right from her. She made sure that he wasn't cheated out of anything when his father's estate was settled, and asked nothing from him in return.

He left the town of Amberton at age 18 with only what he could carry. Everything else he gave to Maria. Leaving her was not easy. She was all he had that came close to family, but the need to avenge his father's death consumed him. He needed to confront the man who'd killed his father as much as he needed food and oxygen. He still remembered Maria in the window as he and Rebel rode slowly by the saloon. He had stopped the horse, but when he turned to wave all he saw was the slight movement of the window curtain. Chase tipped his hat in case she was still watching him. He was headed to the nearest town, Split Rock, in hope of learning something that would help him find his father's killer.

He had inherited his father's guns, a set of beautifully engraved Smith and Wesson Model 3 .44 caliber. He carried the Schofield models in his saddlebags, cleaning them nightly so that they'd be ready when he found his father's killer. The handguns rested in a well-worn leather holster. He'd practiced twice a day for years until the guns became a part of him. He was fast enough, and accurate.

He kicked the remains of the morning campfire, making sure the embers were extinguished as he drank the last of his coffee. He threw his blanket and saddle over Rebel's back, then cinched it down. He packed the tin cup and enameled coffee pot in one of the saddlebags before tying his bedroll behind his saddle.

Rebel softly nickered, alerting Chase the horse was eager to get going. They were heading to Split Rock for supplies and maybe a lead on his father's killer. Rebel needed whole grain. Chase had fed him the last about a week ago. He needed a proper meal himself and maybe even a hot soak in a tub. He reached under his shirt and pulled out a map that he studied briefly before refolding it and tucking it back from where he'd drawn it.

As he swung up into the saddle feeling a sense of excitement. Rebel must have felt it too, because he bucked a little before settling into a canter. He wasn't sure what he'd find in Split Rock -- a peaceful community or a lawless town with ruthless men? He'd find out soon enough. Chase didn't mind putting himself in harm's way, to right a wrong, no matter how long it took. He felt it his duty to stand up to injustice. Cresting a hill, he saw a church steeple, perhaps five miles away. "Won't be long now," he told the horse.

They'd been cantering for quite a while when Rebel reared to a stop, his head jerking to the right. Chase followed his gaze and saw a man dressed in fancy clothes standing in the dried grass, brushing dirt from his clothing. He dismounted and walked over to him.

“You all right, mister?" Chase asked.

“Well, yes I am. I could use some help, though. Something spooked my horse. He threw me clear off and then ran in that direction,” he said, pointing away from town. The man, dressed in a ruffled ascot and a gold-threaded, vest was what Chase called a dandy, a man of means not used to getting his hands dirty. Chase shaded his eyes from the noonday sun and looked toward the nearest stand of trees. He saw a horse silhouetted against the branches.

“Looks like your horse is by those trees. Me and Rebel will get him for you.” Chase got on his horse and headed toward the trees. As they got closer, Rebel slowed to a walk almost as if he sensed the strange horse would run if approached too quickly. Chase gave Rebel his lead, letting him approach and become acquainted with the other horse. After a few minutes, Chase was able to reach out slowly and take the reins. Then they walked the horse back to the man.

“Much obliged. I thank you.” The gentleman said.

“No thanks needed. I’m Chase Mason.” He held his hand out and they shook. The man’s handshake was limp and clammy. Chase noticed his hands were soft, not the calloused mitts of a working man.

"Owen Montgomery," the man pronounced as he handed Chase a business card. "If you ever need anything, come and see me in Split Rock. I owe you, and I always pay my debts."

Chase touched the brim of his hat and tipped his head to the man. "You don't owe me a thing mister. Glad to help. You might want to cinch down those saddle bags before you head out. They're loose."

Montgomery nodded and the two of them divided, heading in different directions.

CHAPTER TWO

Chase rode slowly into town. Rebel was an unusually large horse at 17 hands, pure black with a white stripe down his face. The leather saddle was well worn but in excellent condition. It carried a lasso, bullwhip and two saddle guns in leather holsters that hung over the pommel. One of the two rifle scabbards held a sawed-off 12-gauge shotgun, the other a Winchester .44-40. A blanket roll and saddlebags rode behind him, carrying the essentials for days and nights in the open.

His clothes were coated in trail dust, and Chase noticed the town folk giving him the once over. He saw his reflection in the rippled glass as he passed the general store and didn't blame them. He looked like he meant to cause trouble and had the means to do it. He pulled the dusty bandana from his lower face to make himself look less menacing.

He came to a stop at the stable and dismounted. Holding the reins in one hand, he reached into his pocket with the other. He flipped a quarter to the stable boy, who dropped a shovel of horse manure to catch the coin with both hands.

"Keep my horse fed and watered, and if you clean the saddle, guns and gear I'd be grateful. Be mindful of those saddle guns, both have touchy triggers. Make sure they stay on the saddle; I might have to leave town in a hurry. Horse's name is Rebel. Be careful around his head. He likes to bite until he decides whether or not he likes you."

The boy just nodded, looking as if he were afraid to speak to the trail-dusted stranger.

"Which way to the saloon, kid?"

The boy pointed to a sign that read Empty Glass Saloon, and Chase headed that way, carrying his saddlebags over his shoulder. His legs and back were stiff from riding and he was looking forward to a drink, a decent meal and a hot bath. His size twelve boots scuffed the wooden boards. As he approached the saloon, he heard voices coming from inside. Someone was cussing and calling another a liar and a cheat while others were laughing and having a good time. Piano music filled the air and the bar girls hung on the elbows of the men. Chase stepped through the faded double doors into the stench of sweat, tobacco and stale beer.

As he made his way to the bar, his spurs jangled on the wood plank floor. All conversation and noise had stopped when he entered. He felt every eye on him as he removed his saddlebags and placed them on the bar. Placing one worn boot on the metal footrest, he ordered a whiskey. The barkeep looked nervous, his hands shaking as he poured the drink. Chase raised the shot glass and was about to slug it down when someone shouted, “That’s him right there; he’s the fella was with Owen, outside of town.”

Without any warning, a couple of ragged men grabbed Chase by the elbows. Chase twisted violently and freed his left elbow, which he used to break the nose of one of the men. He stomped on the other’s foot as hard as he could and kneed him in the crotch. The man doubled over in pain, moaning, as he dropped to the floor. Chase turned to put his back against the wall.

“Hold it right there, mister,” a voice bellowed. “I’m the sheriff, and you’re about a rat’s whisker from being shot for what you’ve done.”

The sheriff had pushed through the saloon doors

on a dead run, stopping about six feet from Chase. He leveled a 12-gauge shotgun as he gasped for breath.

"You mind telling me what you think I've done?" Chase asked the sheriff.

"Well, you killed and robbed Owen Montgomery, just about five miles from town. I got a witness that saw you with him while he was still alive and kicking."

"I didn't rob or kill anyone. Why don't we go over to your office and get to the bottom of this?" Chase replied. He knew from past experience it was better to get out of a crowded situation and talk one on one so he could better reason with his accuser. All eyes were on the sheriff as he reluctantly agreed.

"But first, give me that holster with them guns."

Chase slowly unbuckled his gun belt as the sheriff's face twitched.

"Here you go, sheriff. No need to point that gravemaker at me anymore."

The sheriff thought for a bit and then lowered the shotgun, handing it to a man by his side.

"Keep that thing at the ready," he instructed. He took the holster from Chase and slung it over his shoulder.

Chase looked back at the bar keep and said, "I'll be back for those saddlebags. I expect you'll keep them safe for me." The barman nodded, taking the leather bags and putting them under the bar.

The sheriff, the man holding the shotgun and Chase slowly made their way past the saloon patrons to the door. A simmering crowd met them in the street.

"You got a witness, sheriff, and what he done deserves a hanging and you know it," a man who looked to be a blacksmith said. Someone in the crowd threw a rope that landed at the sheriff's feet.

A staggering old man screamed, "We want justice right now, " then promptly passed out, falling face down in the dirt.

Chase could see the sheriff was about to lose control of the mob. He watched him reach down for the rope and hold it high in the air, bellowing, "Let's have us a hanging!"

The sheriff tied a quick noose and tossed it over Chase's head. The crowd screamed its approval. Before the sheriff took two steps toward the lone tree beside the street, a blast stilled the crowd. The stable boy stood in the street, Chase's lever action .44-40 rifle in his shaking hands. Smoke curled slowly from the barrel as the crowd started backing away from the boy, the sheriff and his prisoner, leaving the three of them facing each other.

"What the hell are you doing, you little idiot?" the sheriff screamed. "Put down that rifle right now and get your ass back to the stables where you belong."

The boy's answer was to lever action in another round and point the rifle directly at the sheriff. Chase wheeled around, jerked the rope from the sheriff's hands and tore the noose from his neck.

"I don't much appreciate being judged guilty and set to hang without a fair trial or a chance to explain things." He reached down and removed the lawman's gun from his holster. Chase pointed the pistol at the sheriff's man holding the shotgun. "This be the time to use that thing or hand it over."

The man slowly passed the shotgun to Chase.

"You made the right choice," Chase told the man. He backed over to the stable boy, took his rifle and removed the remaining cartridges. Chase said, "Thanks, kid" and tossed him another quarter. "Now go clean it, since you fired it. I'll hold on to the cartridges." The boy nodded before making his way back to the stable, his face a shade of green.

"What's your name, sheriff?" Chase asked.

"Moore, Tom Moore."

"Ok, Tom. My name is Chase. Let's go to your office and get to the bottom of this."

CHAPTER THREE

The crowd broke into small knots and clumps, lingering to see what would happen next. Chase and the sheriff made their way to the sparse office and Chase kicked the door shut with a dusty boot. He took his own holstered guns from the sheriff. He leaned the shotgun against the wall and buckled on his gun belt. With his two revolvers at his sides he felt more at ease.

"How long you been sheriff? 'Cause I'm guessing you got hired on about yesterday or maybe even this morning. You have no sense of the law and you're about as dumb as a rock. Instead of finding out the facts first, then asking my side of the story, you let that welcoming committee provoke you into something stupid. I should do everyone a favor and shoot you right now."

Now that he saw him hunched behind his desk, Chase found the sheriff frail and pathetic . As he spoke, he barely made eye contact with Chase. "It's not what you think. I had an eyewitness who saw you with Owen outside town. A very reliable witness, I might add."

"Well, let's get that witness in here. We'll have it cleared up in no time. Then I can get back to what brought me here in the first place."

The sheriff got up and turned to face Chase as he spoke. "That person won't be back this way for a day or two. In the meantime, would it be all right with you if you give me my gun back and I lock you up? If people see you walking around town, you'll most likely get shot in the back. It's in your best interest to be behind bars, at least until the witness returns."

Chase glared at the sheriff, causing him to pale. "If you think I'm going in that cell, you're more stupid than you look."

"I can't just let you go. I'd lose my job, and more than likely you'd be dead once that crowd got hold of you. You got any other ideas?"

"I could lock you in a cell and throw away the key. Put on your badge, then go after Owen's killer.

Anyone questions me, I'll tell them you quit and appointed me sheriff until the witness gets back. Or, you can help me. I need to prove that I didn't have anything to do with Montgomery's death," Chase said. "I can tell you that I met Owen Montgomery outside of town, but all I did was help him get his spooked horse back. That means someone else robbed and killed him. You say the witness is honest. I want to know if they claim they saw me commit murder or just assumed I did because I'm a stranger here and was seen with Owen."

The Sheriff quietly responded, "Somebody seen you next to Owen with your arm out, holding something. Could have been a gun."

"The only thing I was holding was his business card. He wanted me to stop by so he could repay me for giving him a hand," Chase replied. "Who is accusing me?"

"Henry G. Hathaway," the sheriff said. "He's in the next town over to attend a hanging."

"Jesus! He accuses a man of robbery and murder, then leaves town to watch someone hang? What kind of person does that? This guy sounds like a real bung hole. Who does he think he is, anyway?"

"He happens to be the judge in these parts," the sheriff said.

"Judge, huh? I didn't notice a courthouse when I rode in."

"We don't have one. Judge Henry G. Hathaway holds court in his private stagecoach. Come to think of it, he hung a man a few days before you rode in."

"What was he guilty of?" Chased inquired.

"Stole a sum a money from Chester Hale, God rest his soul. Killed him for it, too."

"Anyone see him do it? The killing, I mean to say."

"Not sure, but the last person to see old Chester alive was Owen Montgomery. I hear Chester came to town for some bank business a day or so before he was done in."

"Anyone know the killer?"

"Nope. He was a drifter, like you. Some say he rode with the Littlefield gang, over in Long Pine. Robbing banks, stealing horses and killing whoever gets in the way. If you make it out of Split Rock alive, stay the hell away from Long Pine."

"Sounds like the judge got that verdict right. Maybe I do stand a chance once he hears the facts."

"Maybe yes, maybe no. Best you not cause any trouble before the judge gets back. He has no problem handing out a hanging verdict for the smallest offense. All depends on his mood, I reckon."

"What does the G stand for, God?" Chase sneered.

"No," the sheriff replied, "Guilty." The sheriff watched Chase's face, waiting for his reaction.

"Damn, I don't need a madman trying to hang me. I have to find Montgomery's killer before he returns." Chase couldn't leave with an overzealous judge running things. He didn't have a plan yet, but he would figure one out after clearing himself.

"Montgomery have a wife or family here? If he does, I need to convince them that I didn't kill him. Then I can find who did, without everyone in town trying to shoot me."

"The only family left is his daughter, Maggie. She worked alongside him at the bank," the sheriff said.

"How about this? I'll give you back your gun. I'll also get in the cell. But the door stays unlocked. You will get this Maggie here pronto."

The sheriff thought about his options before nodding. He retrieved his handgun and then left the office.

The sheriff could return with the crowd thirsty for vengeance instead of Maggie, but Chase's experience told him he wouldn't. He'd learned plenty about character – and the lack of it – growing up with Maria. He pegged the sheriff as a good man who only wanted quiet and the small steady pay his position brought.

"Nothing to do now, but wait," he said to himself.

As he stretched out, with his boots hanging off the end of the cot, he put his hat over his face and closed his eyes. Chase was just about to nod off when light footsteps on the floorboards outside the door brought him to his feet, ready to let his guns do the talking.

The door slowly opened and a women's hand appeared, clutching a derringer. As she stepped in the room, she pointed it at Chase. The sheriff behind her jumped as she fired the small pistol. The bullet passed harmlessly over Chase's shoulder, lodging in the wall. She turned without a word and shoved past the sheriff, leaving the door open as she ran out crying.

"Maggie, come back here," the sheriff yelled. When she didn't do as ordered, the sheriff turned, closed the door and said, "You're lucky she's not a good shot."

Chase glanced behind him at the bullet in the wall, "So that was Owen's daughter?"

"Yep. I guess that's all she wanted to say to you."

"What did you tell her before you brought her to see me? Come on over to the jail house and meet the man who killed your father?"

"Course not!. I told her I had the last man to see her father alive, is all."

"Thanks for nothing," Chase replied dryly, as he ran his hand through his thick black hair. "Obviously, someone from town told her about me. I still need to talk with her. She may know who would want her father dead." He rose from the cot, walked to the wall where the bullet was half exposed and pried it free. He shoved it in the pocket of his pants. He would add it to the others that were in his saddlebag at the saloon.

"What you doing that for?" the sheriff asked.

"Adding it to my collection of lead that was meant to kill me but didn't. I use it to make new cartridges. Saved me quite a bit of money over the years."

"I'll bet," Moore said softly, then added, "Why do so many people want to shoot you?"

"I'm told I should mind my own business. But I like to help folks who can't help themselves."

Moore looked at Chase, slowly shaking his head. "Mister, you are one of a kind."

Chase hadn't revealed the real reason he collected the lead, but he had told the truth. He believed each bullet fired had a purpose, and that was to wound or kill its intended target. When a bullet missed, it was a wasted shot that should not have been fired. When he eventually fired it from one of his guns, its purpose would be fulfilled.

CHAPTER FOUR

The stable boy spent most of his days mucking stalls, watering horses and filling feed bags. The horses appreciated it, but the owners never did. He'd never received any kind of extra payment for his labor until that blue-eyed stranger came to town. He couldn't explain why he had grabbed the stranger's rifle and stopped the hanging. It was the one time in his life that he acted without thinking about the consequences.

His name was Ben, but most townsfolk called him boy. He lived outside of town in a small but clean cabin with his mother Ruth. His father had left them two years ago to mine gold in California with a promise to return when he'd struck it rich. Ben was certain they would never see him again.

He worked for the stable owner, Lefty Tuttle, for next to nothing because he enjoyed the company of the horses and mules. They were good listeners, and he talked to them about his plans for a better life. They never made fun of him or laughed at his ideas. He worked hard and was exhausted at the end of each day, when he rode his mule Pedro home. There he would do his chores, clean up and enjoy a meager but tasty meal his mother had ready for them. In the morning before work he collected the eggs from the chicken coop, milked the family cow and brought in fresh water to fill the cabin's water barrel.

He put his hand in the pocket of his homespun pants and felt the smooth surface of the silver coins. He moved his fingers to the edge of one and enjoyed the feel of the reeding circumnavigating the rim. He loved the sound they made when he moved them against each other as well and the heft of them in his hand. Ben wanted more of them and he had a plan.

He would take the best care of Rebel that he could, and clean and polish the tack and guns until they looked new. Excited by the thought of pleasing the stranger, he took to the task with a smile. Cleaning the saddle and tack was something he knew, and the boy was pleased when he stepped back to admire his work.

The guns were another matter. Ben could polish

the outside of them but had no idea how to clean and oil them. He needed a gunman's help, so he set off for the saloon. As he made his way around the room, it quickly became apparent that no one was going to offer their assistance. All they did was laugh when he explained what he needed. His head hanging, he scuffed his way toward the door. How was he going to please the stranger when he couldn't even clean a rifle? As he was about to leave, he felt a claw yank him back inside.

"I heard what you were asking folks and I can help you. But I ain't gonna do it for nothing. How much you willing to pay me?" The man reeked of drink and looked mean.

Ben's mind raced, as he pondered the man's question. All he had were the two quarters the stranger had given him. He was desperate, but didn't want to lose both coins in the process.

"I could pay you one quarter, mister."

"How many guns you got needs cleaning?" the man asked.

"A shotgun and a rifle," Ben answered.

"Can't do two guns for only two bits, kid. It's gotta be two quarters, and even that's a bargain. It's gonna take some time to clean them proper."

The thought of losing his precious coins sickened

Ben, but it was the only way to keep his plan going. Then he remembered the drifter saying to keep his saddle guns on the saddle. Maybe he could get a cheaper price for cleaning just the rifle he'd fired. "All right, mister, how about just the rifle. One quarter for one gun. How does that suit you?"

"You just said two guns for twenty-five cents. I don't like you changing the deal. I don't give a damn if it's one or two, the price ain't changing."

Ben knew he had no choice but to accept the deal if he wanted to get them cleaned.

"Ok, mister. Two guns, two quarters. When you want me to get them to you?"

"Now be a good time as any. Wrap them up nice so I have something to cover them with once they get cleaned. I'll be sitting right here when you get back."

"Ok, I'll be back shortly. How long will it take you to clean them?"

"I'll have them ready by the morning after tomorrow. I want to take my time with them because I have a feeling this is important to you. I can even bring 'em to you, if you want."

That would work out best, because he wouldn't miss any more time away from the stable. He had fallen behind in his duties with all the saddle cleaning. He nodded his head and left to retrieve the guns.

He felt uneasy as pulled the long guns from the scabbards and walked back to the saloon. He had never seen the man before but felt he could trust him because the deal was made in full view of everyone at the bar. When he reached the saloon, the man was gone. Ben put the wrapped firearms on a table and sat down to wait for him. He began to worry that he had lost his only chance to have the guns cleaned. He untied and retied the rawhide strip around the bundle five times before the man walked into the saloon.

"Sorry, kid. Had to take care of some other business. Where is my money?"

"Right here. But first I need to know your name. Pa always said you gotta know a man's name if you do business with him."

"You can call me Jax."

"I'm Ben, the stable boy. That's where you can bring them. I'll be there right after sun up, two days from now. Here is a quarter. I'll pay you the rest when I get the guns back."

"Nice try, kid. I'm gonna need payment in full right now 'cause I'm not taking a chance of you not paying me after I done the work. And I'm not going to jail for beating on a

half-wit kid." Jax stuck his hand out, waiting for the money. Ben slowly removed the two coins from his pocket and placed them in the man's outstretched hand. Jax snapped his fingers shut, gathered the covered guns and walked away, saying, "Pleasure doing business, boy. See you soon."

When Ben returned to the stable, he wanted to do more to help the drifter. He was trying hard to figure out how he could help the man clear his name. He stood next to Rebel and said to the horse, "What if I just go tell Miss Montgomery that he didn't do it? I never met the woman nor even been in the bank. Why would she listen to anything I said about the murder?" Rebel stared at the boy and swished his tail. With no ideas in his head, Ben tended to the animals. He shoveled out the manure, and fed and watered the horses as night came on. "I need to get some sleep so I can be here early to get those guns back and surprise him," he mumbled. He couldn't wait to see the look on the stranger's face when he showed him all that he had done.

CHAPTER FIVE

Judge Hathaway stood in the center of Dry Creek and admired his work. His latest case had just ended with a guilty verdict. A lone gunman who had robbed the general store and stolen the owner's horse went chattering to the noose. He would have gotten away with it but for a quick-thinking resident who spooked the stolen horse as it ran by him. The robber was thrown and knocked unconscious.

The Judge smiled as the guilty man's body slowly swayed in the breeze, allowing all who passed to view him. A sign reading "Bank Robber and Horse Thief" had been affixed to his coat. The Judge felt convinced that he had provided justice for the store owner and for the town. It wouldn't do to have word spread that Dry Creek was easy pickings for desperados and miscreants. Hopefully, this would send a clear message.

"Only time will tell," he said to himself.

At the hotel's front desk he announced, "I'll be leaving now and would like my belongings brought to my carriage."

"Certainly, your honor. I'll send someone right up to fetch them," replied the deskman.

"You can send the bill for my stay to the governor. I'm certain he will have no issue paying it."

"Yes sir. Consider it done."

The Judge strutted toward his carriage, which was really a modified stagecoach. He'd had a blacksmith add metal rings to the back of the opposing seat, where prisoners could be chained during sentencing. The upholstery was removed so no comfort would be afforded those on trial. The smith had also devised a small area in the back of the coach that served as a cell – a cage, really -- in the event he had to transport prisoners. It wasn't used much, for the Judge came to guilty verdicts quickly, without a modicum of remorse.

Most miscreants were hung within minutes of his judgement. There was even a pole on the coach that could be swung upright for use as a hanging post if needed. Extra rope, with nooses already tied, were stored under the Judge's padded seat. He employed both.

The Judge noticed the townsfolk watching him as he made his way across town. Most nodded and some even smiled. They appreciated what he had done for Dry Creek. It filled him with conviction that he was justified in handing down death sentences. His verdicts were delivered to defendants as they sat opposite him, most without the benefit of counsel.

It made for quick justice, and that was what was needed in these parts. With so many crimes being committed, time was of the utmost importance. He got in and fumbled for his timepiece.

"Where the hell are my bags? I needed to be on my way to Split Rock five minutes ago," he bellowed, as he leaned out the small curtained window.

"Right here, Judge, right here. We'll have them ready for travel as soon as we lash them down."

"Hurry it up. I have a pressing legal matter. Not only am I the judge for the next trial, I am the only witness."

The two men secured the bags and trunk. One climbed up into the driver's seat, took the reins and released the handbrake. The other grabbed the shotgun and settled next to him. The coachman cracked his whip, yelled "Git" to the four-horse team and the mobile courthouse was on its way. Split Rock was several days away. At some point, they would have to overnight at a stagecoach stop where the Judge could refresh himself and the horses could be properly cared for. Judge Hathaway had made it clear that he must be ready to conduct a trial immediately upon his arrival.

CHAPTER SIX

Chase sat with his back against the cell wall, holding a battered tin cup of black coffee. As he sipped it, he planned his next move. There was no doubt he needed to meet with Maggie, but without getting shot at again. He knew of only two people in town he could ask for help: the sheriff and the stable boy who had saved his neck. The sheriff had failed trying to get Maggie to meet with him, so it might be better to ask a favor of the boy.

"Sheriff, I need you to get word to that stable boy. By the way, what's his name?"

"It's Ben," he replied.

"Tell him I need to talk to him about my horse. I have a feeling those animals are his life, so he won't hesitate to come."

"I'll go fetch him, the sheriff said. "You remember to stay in that cell." He slammed the door shut behind him.

"Jesus, now I'm his little errand boy." Sheriff Moore didn't think Chase Mason killed Owen, but because the Judge said he did, he was in a tough spot. He liked Chase, but he couldn't set him free without incurring the wrath of Judge Hathaway. All Sheriff Moore really wanted was to be left alone. The sheriff studied the street. Things were pretty much back to normal, though he did note curtains rustling in several windows as he made his way across town to the stable.

"Someone's always watching," he muttered as he entered the stable. He found Ben pushing a wheelbarrow of manure, and gruffly told him to get his behind to the office and wait there.

"No need me explaining things to that dimwit," he said to himself as the boy left. He noticed the gleaming bridle the boy had just hung up.

"Jesus, that's sure a damn sight better treatment than I got when I stabled my horse here awhile back. I guess being the sheriff doesn't buy me a thing in this Godforsaken town."

He grabbed a shovelful of manure from the wheelbarrow and flung it toward the gleaming bridle, covering it in horse shit.

"Guess you're not quite done, kid" he chuckled.

WHEN BEN ENTERED the sheriff's office, he was surprised to find the cell door open and the stranger sipping from a tin cup. He came to an abrupt stop, not really sure what to do.

"Hello, Ben. I need to ask a favor of you."

"Sure thing. What is it, mister?"

"I need to talk to Maggie over at the bank, but she isn't willing to see me. Can you bring her a note before she leaves the bank this afternoon?"

"Pa says I should know a man's name before doing business with him."

"Smart man, your pa. My name is Chase, Chase Mason."

"Ok, I'll do that and anything else you might need me for." Ben smiled. "This is the most exciting thing that's happened since I got kicked by my mule."

Chase removed Owens' business card from his shirt pocket and walked over to the sheriff's desk. There he rummaged around, looking for something to write with.

Just as he was about to open one of the drawers, the sheriff returned.

“What the hell you doing in my desk? Get away from there, mister. You got no right searching through another man’s belongings. Especially, if he’s the sheriff. Get back in the cell where you belong. That’s the deal you made, and I expect you to stick to it.”

“Sorry, sheriff, you’re right. I should have waited to ask, but you were gone and I'm going to be tried for murder as soon as the judge gets back. That being what it is, I don’t have time to wait around. I need to clear my name as soon as possible.” Chase headed back to the cell and sat down. He took a bullet out of his pocket, putting it on the back of his fingers. Moving his fingers, he watched it dance its way across, then back again. This was something he did to help him focus.

“I need Ben to pass along a note to Maggie so I can meet with her.”

“What would you write that would cause her to act any different than she did before?”

“I didn’t kill her father.”

“We already tried a meeting and it didn’t work out. Ben, you get back to the stable. I’m sure you have work that needs doing. There will be no note passing.”

Ben looked at the tall, dark-haired man for direction and Chase nodded. Before Ben left, Chase asked him how Rebel was doing. Ben said, “He may not want to leave, he’s being treated so good.”

Chase was running out of time. He got up from the uncomfortable plank seat and started pacing the cell. He had to figure a way to get out of the trouble he was in before the Hanging Judge returned.

CHAPTER SEVEN

Maggie finished her paperwork, rubbed her tired eyes and glanced around the bank. Without her father there to help, she had to do everything. Even when he was alive, it was a long day, taking care of the banking business. She didn't know how much longer she could do this alone.

The funeral service was over before she could close out all his business transactions and estate, not to mention the house chores, laundry and cooking.

I'm so angry with myself for missing the shot I took. Why didn't I take more bullets with me? I won't get my life back until that murdering bastard gets what's coming to him, she thought.

She didn't care for hangings, avoiding them at all cost. This time would be different. That man in the cell needed to pay for what he'd done. Maybe she would buy a new outfit, something nice and bright. She wanted everyone to notice her there, especially that murdering drifter. Judge Hathaway might even let her stand real close, maybe even pull the lever that sends the evil man back to Hell.

Darkness fell as she was locking the bank door. She heard heavy footsteps coming her way. Nervously fumbling with the key, she managed to get it locked just as a man came up behind her. As she turned to see who it might be, a bolt of panic ran through her. This couldn't be a regular customer because; someone would have hailed a greeting before getting this close.

A cloth bag was thrown over her head. Before she could scream, a voice growled, "If you don't stay quiet, I'll kill you right here."

She remained silent but couldn't stop shaking. Bile burned the back of her throat, making breathing difficult, and the man held the bag tight around her throat.

"What do you want?" she managed to whisper.

"Listen up now and listen good. I'm gonna need the paper for the land my mine is on. I paid Owen the money that was owed on it, but he never give me the claim. Open that damn door and get me what's mine."

Maggie didn't have a clue what the man was talking about.

"Why don't you come back in the morning when the bank is open and I'll help you? I can open early, if that is satisfactory," she rasped.

The man hissed, "Get that door open now or die. I don't have time to waste."

He pressed her against the door and tightened his grip on her throat. Maggie had no choice but to open the door, so she fumbled in her handbag for the key and somehow managed to get it in the lock, even though she couldn't get her hands to stop shaking.

Inside the bank, the man threw her to the floor hard enough to stun her and ran to Owens' office. It sounded like he was rummaging through the drawers and the bookcase, even opening books, looking for the claim. Maggie slowly cleared her head then carefully lifted the cloth bag enough to see the man. As he looked behind the framed certificates on the wall, she tried to memorize his face. He wasn't from the town. She slid the bag back down as he stumbled out of the office, out of breath and cursing.

"You need to get me that paper. Bring it to me tomorrow at sundown. I'll be waiting down by the creek, by the big rock with the split in it. If you want to live, you'll be alone. And don't say a word about this to anyone. Nod if you understand."

She nodded, then said, "I need to know your name

or the name of the mine so I can locate it. I don't know anything about my father holding paper for a mine."

"You must think I'm stupid. I ain't telling you my name. The name on the claim is Chester Hale. Remember, sundown or I'll pay you another visit. And I won't be as nice to you as I was today."

He stepped over her, leaving the bank without closing the door.

"Keep the bag as a reminder," he growled over his shoulder.

CHAPTER EIGHT

Maggie, scared and confused, slowly got up from the floor. She had no idea what the stranger had referred to. It was time to involve the sheriff.

She straightened her clothes and limped to the sheriff's office. Maybe the sheriff would recognize the man. When she opened the door she was shocked to see the man she'd taken a shot at out of the cell and drinking coffee. She was about to flee when she heard the sheriff's voice command her to come in.

She completely forgot about being attacked at the bank. "What about him?" she shrieked. "Why isn't he in the cell where he belongs? And why is he wearing his gun belt?"

Maggie wished she had brought along her derringer

again so she could finish what she'd started. She did the next best thing, grabbing the enameled coffee pot from the cast iron stove beside the door. She hurled it at the tall man as he walked toward her. He ducked, easily avoiding it and the pot hit the wall. Maggie cowered behind the sheriff.

"He's going to kill me, just like he did my father! Shoot him, sheriff. It's self-defense."

"No one is gonna shoot anyone," the sheriff said. "Sit down and listen to the facts."

Maggie reluctantly obliged, huddling close to the sheriff.

"Take a seat, Chase. Now is the time to let this woman know your account of what happened between you and her father before you rode into town."

Chase obliged, holding the tin cup in his oversized hands as his striking blue eyes looked directly into Maggie's. "First off, my name is Chase Mason. I know your name is Maggie and you're Owen's daughter. I'm sorry for your loss, but I want you to know that I had absolutely nothing to do with his murder. In fact, I have to find the killer to clear my name before I can leave this damn town. I have my own business to attend to."

Maggie was surprised at the stranger's words. She had expected an uncivilized murderer, the dregs of the streets with no conscience. But he sounded sincere. Now she didn't know what to think.

"I suppose I should hear your account of that day before I ask the judge to pull the lever that hangs you," she said reluctantly.

Now it was Chase's turn to be shocked. He was not expecting her to care about anything he said. "Well, miss, all I can do is tell you my side of the story."

He spent the next few minutes recounting what had happened earlier that day. He also showed her the business card Owen had handed him before they separated.

"Well, Maggie, I gotta say, it sounds possible," the sheriff said when Chase stopped speaking. "There is no real evidence this man did it. All I have to go on is what the judge said happened. If he did murder your father, why would he come into town? He would be the logical suspect. It don't make no sense. I'm keeping him in here so he doesn't get shot by some drunken idiot looking for vengeance."

It was a lot to take in and Maggie was already overwhelmed by her attack at the bank. She had originally wanted to kill Chase, but now she might need his help. She felt woozy as she tried to stand. Her head hit the side of the desk as she fainted.

"I'll go get Doc Hodge. Put her in the cell and cover her with a blanket. I'll be right back."

Chase easily lifted Maggie and carefully placed her on the rope bed as gently as he could. He placed a blanket under her head and one over her. He noticed some blood dripping from her forehead, so he wet his handkerchief and carefully wiped it off.

The door flew open and the sheriff and doctor stormed in. The doctor took one look at Maggie and decided to get her over to his office where he could attend to her. With a head injury, he told the sheriff, it was best he watch her closely for a few days.

Chase picked Maggie up, and said, "Let's get her to your office."

"Okay, mister, follow me. It's not far."

"You're gonna get shot at if anyone sees you," the sheriff yelled.

"I have more serious things to worry about." Chase went out the door without closing it behind him.

At the doctor's office, Chase followed him into a room with a small bed. The doctor motioned for Chase to put Maggie on the bed. . He didn't realize Maggie was awake, so when she spoke it surprised him.

"Please don't go just yet. I have something of great importance to tell you."

"I think it can wait 'til tomorrow, don't you?"

"No, I don't. If you leave without listening to what I have to say I'll get up and follow you back to the sheriff's office. I might anyway, because I don't need the doctor hovering over me like a sick child when I'm not injured."

"Listen here, Miss Montgomery. You are not going to leave this room before I examine you and that's final. Your father, God rest his soul, would be terribly upset if I allowed that," the doctor replied sternly.

Maggie sank back on the bed. "All right, Doc. I'll do as you say. But I must speak with Chase before he goes."

"That's fine. Just keep it short and don't get up." The doctor left the room to give them some privacy. Chase went to the side of the bed, wondering what the woman had to say that was so damn important.

"First thing is, I'm not completely sure you are innocent. I agree with the sheriff that it doesn't make sense that you came into town if you did murder my father."

As the last words were spoken, Maggie stifled a sob but continued.

"If the sheriff thinks you didn't do it and there is no proof, I have no other choice but to go with what my instincts tell me." Maggie composed herself, looked at Chase and said, "I must apologize for my earlier actions, but at the time I believed they were justified. I have since changed my mind. I believe you did not kill my father. Perhaps working together, we can help each other."

Maggie told Chase about her attacker at the bank and what he sought.

"It seems likely that Owen was killed for what that man wants. And you might be next.

Whoever is behind this is not fooling around. Do you think you can find the claim?" Chase asked.

"I'm not sure. It may be hidden at the house. As soon as the doctor lets me, I'll start looking for it."

"Let's hope he finds nothing serious. Every minute we sit here, we're burning daylight doing nothing. It will be sundown before you know it."

When Maggie nodded, it did cause her some discomfort. *Maybe I'm more injured than I thought.*

CHAPTER NINE

Chase left the doctor's office and decided to check on Rebel. He made his way to the stable by moving from shadow to shadow. He knew how to move without being seen.

The sliding door resisted at first, but yielded when he put his back into it. He closed it behind him and halted a minute for his eyes to adjust to the dim interior. The smell of fresh hay, oats and horses was like the smell of a home-cooked meal. He gave a short whistle and Rebel responded with a whinny. Chase looked down the row of stalls, quickly seeing his horse staring at him with ears pricked forward.

He took stock of Rebel, was impressed with Ben. Chase had never seen the horse's coat shine as it did.

The boy must have spent hours brushing him. Rebel pushed his head against Chase and nickered.

"Hey boy, I've missed you," Chase told him, as he rubbed the horse's muzzle. Chase took in the horse's scent and feel of his hide, immediately feeling the urge to saddle up and move on; go somewhere that was nowhere near this town. Practice with his guns during the day and sit by a campfire at night. No accusations of murder or threats of hanging. Just he and Rebel, following the trail of his father's killer.

Instead, he was stuck in Split Rock, accused of murder by a hanging judge, who seemed more than eager to err on the side of the noose. A sense of urgency flooded through him, causing his scalp to tingle. "See you soon, fella," he said to Rebel, as he headed for the door. On his way out, he noticed Rebel's bridle hanging on a wooden peg, covered with horse shit.

Sure, Ben had taken great care of his horse, but he'd neglected everything else. Chase had no time to check the rest of his gear. He made a mental note to confront Ben in the morning and left for the sheriff's office.

Chase entered the sheriff's office and strode to the desk. He looked down at the sheriff and growled, "I can't stay here any longer. I need to be out there tracking down the killer."

"I hear what you're saying, but it's not safe for you to go roaming around. You'd be shot, probably in the back, as soon as one of the locals seen you."

"What if you were with me? They wouldn't shoot then, would they?"

"Likely not, but I can't make no promises. You'd be taking one hell of a risk."

"I would rather take the risk than be hung in the street."

Sheriff Moore looked skeptical. "I need to know what you're up to before I agree to piss off a bunch of people, including the judge."

"Maggie has a meeting with a man at sundown who might be connected to Owen's

murder. I plan to tag along and make sure she isn't harmed. Maybe I can force the man to talk."

"I bet you're good at that. So now you and Maggie are friends? How in hell did that happen?"

"Let's just say she asked for my help and I couldn't refuse."

"Even though she shot at you and wants to see you swinging in the wind?"

"Someone roughed her up and threatened her. I intend to make sure he never thinks of it again."

"Don't worry, you won't have to do much," Chase continued. "All you need to do is get me safely to the edge of town. Then you can run back to your desk and pretend everything is fine. Later you can follow up on Owen's murder and find the real killer."

"Waste a time," the sheriff said. "The only witness is Judge Hathaway. No one dares to go against him."

"Suit yourself. I won't be coming back here after I help Maggie. Thanks for protecting me from the mob. It would be a shame if I was dead before my phony trial and hanging."

Chase's words irritated the sheriff. He knew he was under the judge's thumb but didn't like to have it shoved in his face. All he could do now was to help the stranger and hope he found the real killer before Hathaway returned. The sheriff didn't need an angry hanging judge looking to pay him back for ruining the public spectacle planned for the stranger. His chair scraped the wooden floor as he got up and walked to the drifter.

"Gimme your gun belt. You can't be seen wearing it while with me. You'll get it back when we get you where you need to be."

Chase reluctantly obliged. He felt vulnerable. The sheriff slung the belt over his shoulder, turned and motioned for Chase to follow.

They weren't far from the sheriff's office when a group of men burst from the saloon, hooting and hollering. One of them drew his gun and started firing at windows in the hotel. Soon all of them were firing at the windows.

"What the hell," the sheriff sputtered. "I'm gonna have to go over there and put a stop to that. You're on your own now."

Before he could take a step, one of the men saw Chase and motioned to the others. The shooting caused Chase and the sheriff to take cover. The sheriff handed Chase his guns and said, "I don't want to be responsible for you getting killed."

Chase strapped on the guns. "If you hide here long enough they'll run out of bullets. Then you can run back to the office and wait for that judge of yours to tell you what to do."

He abruptly turned away, leaving the sheriff to deal with the drunken men, who were now staggering back into the saloon.

CHAPTER TEN

Doc Hodge examined Maggie. He felt her head, feeling for bumps or bruises. He cleaned the blood from her face and looked into her eyes with a magnifier. He asked her a few simple questions, which she answered immediately. He had her stand and walk forward and then close her eyes and raise her arms as high as she could and then walk backward a few steps.

"Maggie, it looks like you're fine. No obvious effects from hitting your head. You'll have some bruising and soreness, but that's to be expected. You can go now, but if you feel you're not yourself in a couple days come back and I'll take another look. You should be fine, just take it easy."

"Thank you, doctor. I appreciate you treating me on short notice."

"Come, come, my dear. It was an emergency. And besides, I had no other patients this afternoon. Have a good afternoon."

Maggie slowly headed home, her body resisting every step. She wanted to take a hot bath and change her clothes.

"I need to find that damn claim first," she muttered. There might not be time for a hot bath after all.

She sighed at the thought. The step up onto the porch seemed much higher as she made her way to the front door. Unlocking it, she went in and felt a sense of panic overtake her.

What if I can't locate the claim? That man will come back and surely hurt or even kill me, she thought. Tears ran down her face as she collapsed into her father's favorite chair. After sobbing for a minute or two, she looked up at the framed silhouette of her father hanging on the wall. Just seeing his profile filled her with the resolve to find his killer.

She wiped her eyes with the sleeve of her dress, rising out of his chair to change her clothes. She hurt all over. Maybe a sip of whiskey would do. Whenever her father had stiffness or soreness, or even a bad day, that's what he did.

She had never had a drink in her life and had

always scolded her father when he did. With no second thought, she pulled the stopper from the decanter and filled a small delicate glass. As she lowered the decanter, a yellowed piece of paper fell from the bottom of it, floating to the floor. Maggie returned the decanter and stooped to pick up the paper while holding the glass of whiskey. Why would her father, a meticulous man and record keeper, put anything like that under the decanter?

She unfolded the paper and read it. Instead of a small sip, she gulped the drink down and coughed violently. Barely able to take a breath, she wondered why anyone would think a drink of whiskey was good medicine. After changing her clothes, Maggie made sure her derringer was loaded.

She needed to show Chase the note before he headed to the creek.

As Maggie gathered herself, her sadness turned to excitement. Now she was helping find her father's killer.

CHAPTER ELEVEN

Judge Hathaway was irritated. The hostler at the stagecoach stop noticed that one of the horses had thrown a shoe. He didn't mention to the Judge that he could easily replace the shoe. He despised the Judge for a variety of reasons and wouldn't be helping him. It would be sometime tomorrow before the farrier could tend to the horse.

"Damnation", Hathaway muttered. "If it isn't one thing it's another. Now I'll be a day or so late for the trial in Split Rock."

The Judge was convinced there was no excuse for him or anyone else to miss a court date. The only way out of this situation was clearly evident. He had to change the date of his arrival. He needed to ensure the sheriff held the prisoner and not let some drunken fool shoot him. He prepared a message.

The Judge was a frequent visitor at the stagecoach stop. He even enjoyed his own private room. He never had to pay because the owner of the inn was in some bad trouble awhile back, and Judge Hathaway made the trouble vanish.

He entered the inn to inquire if anyone was headed to Split Rock. He was certain a man with his reputation would have no trouble finding a rider to deliver his urgent message to the sheriff. He ordered the innkeeper to ask around while he made his way to his room. Once there, he freshened up before heading for his dining area.

As soon as he was seated, Judge Hathaway bellowed, "Millie, bring me some of that delicious johnnycake. And be sure to slather on some of those beans and salt pork. And some coffee to wash it down with."

"Yes, sir ... coming right up, your honor."

Millie rushed to deliver his food. The woman knew all about Henry and what he expected. About a year or so ago he'd stopped and ordered the exact same thing. The inn was at full capacity then, so Millie was slow in serving his meal. As soon as she put the plate on the tavern table, he'd pushed it to the floor. She was shocked by his action, but immediately cleaned up the mess and brought him another plate of food. As soon as she put it on the table, he again pushed it to the floor. This happened one more time before he accepted the meal and consumed it. She learned then never to be slow getting his meal or anything else he demanded.

Millie placed the meal on the table and poured a full cup of coffee for him.

"Anything else, your honor?"

"No, this will be all."

"Hope you like it."

The Judge dismissed her with a wave of his portly hand and began eating. Millie retreated, smiling to herself. He would never know that each time she served him she ladled in a little something from the saloon spittoon. Just her way of paying him back for his behavior.

After eating, the judge ambled over to the bar, where a drink appeared immediately. He liked his whiskey, but only the finest available. No Prairie Dew or Applejack for him. A man of his importance would not drink the common swill, nor with the common folk. He walked with his whisky in hand, making his way to the innkeeper's office.

“So, did you find anyone I can pay to deliver a message in Split Rock?”

“Yes, Judge, I did. This man will be leaving as soon as you reach an agreement with him. Who is it you want him to give it to once he gets there?”

“Give it to the sheriff. Impress upon this messenger that urgency is required and expected.”

The Judge removed a note from his vest pocket and handed it to the innkeeper.

“I’ll pay him ten dollars -- after I know the note was delivered.”

“I’ll let him know the details. That’s him outside getting ready to ride. Name’s Emmett Blackman. He’ll be expecting payment upon your return to town.”

“Of course, of course. No worries there. By the way, next time I ask you for something it better be you coming to me. I had to walk all the way here from the bar. Completely unacceptable.”

The Judge turned away, waddling to his room with some difficulty. He was dog tired and ready for sleep. Tomorrow would involve a long day of travel. The upcoming murder trial needed resolution quickly to restore respect for the law and to show all that punishment was swift in his jurisdiction. He would not allow anyone to challenge his law. He was snoring within minutes.

CHAPTER TWELVE

Ben couldn't sleep, thinking how pleased the stranger would be. When he arrived at the stable, he could barely slide the big door open, he was so tired. Daylight was just beginning to make an appearance and the stabled animals were letting him know they were hungry. He stumbled around, barely able to complete the morning chores. When he finished, he sat down on a hay bale to rest.

The boy looked around, noticing the sunlight coming through the cracks and holes of the old barn. He loved the way he could see the dust and pieces of hay floating in the light. Ben could not stop his eyes from closing as he listened to the comforting sound of the horses eating.

He was rudely awakened by rough hands shaking

him. It wasn't Jax, it was the stranger. Ben felt sickened as Chase demanded to know where his guns were. Ben tried to explain what happened, but instead of words, all he could get out was a burp and dry heave. He was terrified as he looked at Chase's imposing outline with the sunlight behind him. The man's blue eyes seemed to glow as he growled.

"Where the hell are my guns?"

"I don't have them right now, but I will soon," the boy stammered.

"Kid, you'd better tell me right now what's going on. I need those guns."

Chase looked down at Ben, knowing that if the stable boy were a grown man he would have beaten him near to death. He wasn't going to hurt the kid, so he realized he would have to take things much easier.

"Look, I'm angry, but you need to explain things so I can get them back. Don't worry, I won't hurt you."

Chase moved toward Ben, and as he did, Rebel saw him and nickered. Chase changed direction, heading to the horse. As he walked to the stall, he said over his shoulder, "Be back in a bit. I gotta talk to my horse."

Chase knew the boy would relax a little if he gave him a moment to make his mouth work.

After visiting with Rebel, Chase sat next to Ben on the bale of hay.

"Ok, kid. Spill your guts. I'm all ears."

Ben was afraid to look at the stranger as he recounted his plan to care for Rebel, the saddle, tack and the guns.

"Mr. Mason, I just wanted you to be extra satisfied. I took care of everything myself except

for cleaning them guns. I can do an all right job on them, but I wanted them to be like new for you."

"Who did you give them to? I suppose it's a local man you know well? So it will be easy to get them back."

Ben could barely get the words out.

"Never saw the man before. He was sitting in the saloon when I went there to ask if anyone could help me. He said his name was Jax. I paid him four bits to do the job.

He was supposed to bring them here this morning."

Chase couldn't believe what he'd just heard. He wanted to pick the boy up and throw him through the barn wall. Instead, he said, "Tell me exactly what he looked like and anything else you remember about him. I need to find him right away."

Ben described the man as best he could remember. He added that the man reeked of drink, so maybe he was at the saloon right now.

"Stick with me, kid. I'm gonna need you to point him out as soon as you see him. We'll start at the saloon."

Ben was both scared and excited. Maybe he could still please the stranger after all. If he could just identify the thief, things would be made right.

Chase and the boy headed to the saloon.

"First sign of trouble, kid, get behind me. I don't need you getting killed. I got enough trouble to deal with."

They reached the swinging doors and stepped slowly into the dimly lit saloon. It was strangely

quiet, even for this time of the day. The barkeep was wiping down the bar while a few of the ladies of the evening picked up broken glass and cleaned the small tables. Chase strode to the bar.

"Howdy, mister. I was wondering if you know where Jax is. It's important that I find him right now."

The bartender recognized Chase from the other day. His hands shaking, he replied, "Can't say as I do. He's not from around here, but he did state he had a little business to take care of in town."

"Was he here last night?"

"Don't recall seeing him lately. Last time I did, he was talking to that stable boy you got with you."

"So did you see him leave that night? Overhear

anything or see something that might help me find him?"

"Nope, all I know for certain is he left carrying a wrapped bundle. The kid was asking if someone would clean a few guns for him. Maybe Jax offered to do that. Why don't you ask the kid?"

"Already did. Just wanted to see if you knew something different."

The barkeep didn't dare ask the stranger how he got out of jail. All he knew for sure was the drifter being here meant trouble wasn't far behind.

"Thanks for your time. One more thing, if I had some guns to sell, anybody in town be interested in buying them?"

"Only one person I can think of. Maybe Walt Young. He owns the mercantile. Sells guns and ammo. Could be he buys them, too. If the price is right."

"Thanks for your time, I appreciate it."

Chase wheeled around, almost knocking Ben down.

"Let's go. Maybe Jax is still there haggling for more money."

Ben started running as fast as he could in the direction of the store. Chase followed him, and when they reached the door he pulled the boy back and told him to stay put.

“How will you know it’s Jax if you never saw him before?”

“Don’t worry, kid. I’ll know my guns when I see them.”

Ben felt ill as he sat on the edge of the wooden sidewalk. How could he have been so stupid?

Chase entered the mercantile, every part of him ready for a fight. Moving quietly, he saw no one. He made his way slowly to a corner of the room. With his back against the wall, he yelled out: “Walt, you here? I need to talk to you about buying some guns.”

No answer and no movement. It was as quiet as a graveyard on payday Friday. As Chase was about to rejoin the stable boy, a side door opened and a man appeared.

“Sorry, mister. Had to use the privy out back. What can I do you for?”

“I’m interested in some guns you might have. I was wondering if you have any used ones for sale.”

“Today might be your lucky day. I just received in my inventory some real nice ones. Come on

to the back room and I’ll show you what I have.”

Chase followed Walt to another room that had a padlocked door. The man took out a key ring and found the key to unlock it.

“Stay here until I get some lanterns lit. I boarded

up the windows for security and now it's too dark to really see anything."

Chase waited as Walt lighted the lamps.

"Come on in, mister. Now you can see what I have. By the way, you know my name but I don't know yours."

"Name's Mason. I see the pegs on the wall, but no guns. Where are they?""

"Nice to meet you, Mr. Mason. I was sold out until just this morning. Fella came in and sold me some. I haven't had time to hang them yet."

Walt went to a wooden crate and opened the snipe-hinged lid. He removed a bundle and brought it to the worn table where Chase stood waiting. He watched as Walt untied the rawhide straps from the cloth covering and unveiled the contents.

The guns were not his.

Without a word to the storekeeper, Chase wheeled around and left the room. He went outside and pulled Ben by the elbow into the room.

"Kid, describe the man you had dealings with to Walt. I don't have any more time to waste here."

"Hi, Mr. Young."

"Hello, Ben. Go ahead, son, I'm listening."

Ben started to explain the whole story, but Chase

cut him off. "Just describe the man. I need those guns this morning."

Ben did as he was told. After he'd finished, Walt immediately said, "That's the man I bought the guns from all right. But he said his name was Ben. Told me he was just passing through and needed money."

Chase asked, "Did you happen to ask him where he was from?"

"No. Not really my business," replied the shop keep.

Ben responded, "He told me his name was Jax. I met him over at the saloon. He didn't say anything about going anywhere to me. He was supposed to clean the guns and bring them to me."

Chase could tell that Walt was not lying to him. But he did have one more question for the clerk: "How much did you give the man for those guns, anyway? In case I want to sell you mine someday."

"Ten dollars is what I paid the man."

Chase knew that no one would let their guns go at that price. Now he knew for certain that Jax had kept his guns and sold his own.

"Come on, kid. Time's a wasting."

They left the store. When Ben dared to, he looked at Chase. He didn't even appear upset. "Mister, why ain't you hopping mad about everything?"

Chase replied, "Never smart going off half-cocked. Makes more sense to slow down and sort things out. Let's get to the stable so I can figure out my next move."

Ben feared the man but admired him at the same time. Chase could hurt him at the barn, but Ben followed him anyway. The boy was determined to help Chase find Jax. They entered the stable and Chase pointed to Rebel's bridle without saying a word. Ben looked over and then ran to it. He started cleaning off the horse shit as if his life depended on it.

CHAPTER THIRTEEN

After leaving the sheriff's office without seeing the stranger or the sheriff, Maggie decided to go to the creek on her own. Apparently this Chase Mason was not a man of his word. Or maybe he had something to do with all that gunfire she'd heard. She had to meet the man at the creek, so she couldn't wait for Chase any longer.

She had her derringer and planned to use it before her attacker hurt her again. Searching both the house and the bank to find a hidden claim would take days. She was certain the paper from her father's office wasn't what the man had demanded, but it would do to hand him so that she could shoot him while he read it.

As Maggie walked toward the meeting place,

Chase Mason was on her mind. *What had brought him to Split Rock in the first place? He'd explained how he met Owen, but not why he'd come to town. Something to ask him later,* she thought. Maggie came to the end of town and stepped off the wooden sidewalk. As she was about to take another step, strong arms went around her and pulled her backward into the alley by the stable.

"Jesus wept, woman, where do you think you're going? Chase demanded.

Maggie almost fainted when he grabbed her. It took some time before she could answer.

"When I couldn't find you or the sheriff, I decided to go to the meeting alone."

"Are you trying to get yourself killed? Because that's one sure way to do it. How did you see the meeting playing out?"

"I was going to shoot the bastard when I handed him the paper."

"So you found what he was looking for?"

"No, it's just a note on old yellowed paper that I found at the house."

"So you hand him something that's going to rile him. Then what?"

"Then I shoot him with this." Maggie rummaged in her handbag and finally removed the derringer.

"That's a one-shot pea shooter. What if you miss? You have any more cartridges with you?"

"I don't."

"Ever shot a man?"

"No, but I did shoot at you. So I know if I'm angry enough I can do it."

"Well, Maggie, you missed me and I wasn't even expecting it. This fella is going to be on a hair trigger and willing to kill you to boot. Why go there alone when I said I would help you?"

"I don't really know you, so I wasn't sure you meant what you said."

"But you believe me when I say I didn't kill your father."

"Yes."

"My horse makes more sense than you do. Either you trust me or you don't. There is no middle ground here. Good thing I saw you from the stable when you walked by. Otherwise you would have been hurt bad or even killed."

What Chase said was true. How could I have decided to go it alone? she thought.

"I'm sorry. It's a bad plan. I should have waited for you, but I panicked. Or it could have been the whiskey."

"You've been drinking? Another bad decision."

"Look here, I'm sorry I didn't wait. And I never had a drink before, but for some reason it seemed the right thing to do. Good thing I did, too, because that's how I found this."

Maggie handed him the folded paper. He read it and then asked, "Is that the Judge's handwriting?"

"It must be. He signed it."

"Well, that means two things. We have a reason why your father was killed." Chase paused a bit before adding, "And now we have a suspect. The only other person known to see Owen the day he was murdered was Judge Hathaway."

"Yes, but how can we prove he did it? All we have is the note. You're a drifter and he's a judge. Why would anyone believe us?"

"Maggie, I don't know how we're going to do it. All I know is we have something to go on and that I didn't kill Owen. Someone else did and I'm going to find him."

"But that doesn't have anything to do with a claim for a gold mine or why I was attacked."

"Maybe, maybe not. You sure you don't remember anything about a land transfer or purchase involving your bank?"

"I'm sure. All loans for land acquisitions I handle. Land transfers would be done at the Assayer's Office.

Either way, I would have heard about a gold mine changing hands. This is a small town with no secrets. Everyone likes to gossip as soon as they know something."

"All towns have their secrets."

Like the fact that the Hanging Judge wrote an I.O.U. to Owen for ten-thousand dollars, Chase thought. At least now he had a course of action. First, though, he needed to deal with the man who had roughed up Maggie.

"Let's get going, Maggie. We have somewhere to be at sundown." Chase took Maggie's arm and turned her back toward town.

"Wait," she protested. "We need to go the other way."

"We won't be going anywhere near the meeting place. He might have extra men there. You're going back to the bank and work late into the night."

"But that mean snake of a man will come looking for me like he said he would."

"Right. I want him to. That's how we catch him without you getting killed. Don't worry, I'll be in the bank. He won't hurt you. I can't wait to get my hands on the bastard."

Maggie's earlier plan to shoot her assailant was foolhardy.

What was I thinking? It must have been the whiskey, she thought. Going to the bank so the man would come to her was a much better plan. This Chase would protect her and she would find out who was behind all of this and why.

"I agree with your plan. It seems like a good one compared to what I was going to do."

She smiled at Chase after she spoke and waited for him to smile back. But his face was set with grim determination and his stride purposeful. She struggled to keep up, glad she'd worn her boots.

CHAPTER FOURTEEN

Emmett Blackman rode into town, dismounted at the saloon and went in for a drink. He was parched from the ride. He knew he should deliver the message right away, but a drink and a bit of rest from the saddle would set him right. His first drink went down easy. He ordered the barkeep to pour him another. As he sipped the cheap whiskey, one of the ladies of the establishment sat next to him.

"Hello, Emmett. Would you all like to buy me a drink and talk a spell? I'm kind of lonely, just saying."

"Why sure, Betty Sue. I'd be pleased to."

He'd visited the saloon a time or two, but never got this close to one of the ladies. Though he knew the names of the girls, he was more interested in playing poker and drinking then spending time with them. He gave the bartender a nod toward the woman and a glass of whiskey arrived for her.

"Thank you, sir. I surely appreciate your kindness to a troubled girl like me."

"Why, what kind of trouble could a beautiful girl like you be in?"

"Well, Emmett, it seems my rent is due and I have no means to pay it."

The young girl leaned into Emmett, her ample breasts rubbing against him. She put one arm around his neck and started to sob.

"I just don't know what to do. If I can't pay, I can't stay. Can you think of anything that would help me out of this terrible mess?"

Emmett wasn't married and didn't have a girlfriend. When Betty Sue leaned against him

he decided he would help her. He would have some extra money when the Judge paid for the delivery of his message.

"I can help you, but it will be a day or two before I have the money. By the way, how much we talking about?"

The girl immediately stopped sobbing and started kissing him.

"Thank you, thank you, thank you! I can't believe my prayers have been answered.

Let's go to my room so we can figure out how much I'm short. I'm good with some things but numbers ain't one of them."

"Okay, but first I got to string a line. I've been riding for hours."

After he downed his drink and left to relieve himself, Betty Sue said, "Johnny, send a bottle of the good stuff to my room. Looks like I'll be busy for the night. When he comes back, give him my room number. Oh, and don't forget to put everything on his tab."

"Girl, you really know how to work them. I'll see to it."

When Emmett returned, the barman told him her room number. He climbed the winding stairs and found his way to the room. As he entered, the first thing he saw was Betty Sue laying naked on the bed. He closed the door, forgetting all about the message.

He woke the next day with a whopping hangover, naked and with no recollection of the night. Betty Sue was still sleeping. He tried unsuccessfully to wake her. She mumbled something he didn't understand and turned on her stomach. He looked around the room and saw the empty whiskey bottle on the night stand.

"What the hell did I get myself into this time?" he

muttered. His head pounding, he slowly dressed and left.

I'll say goodbye to Betty Sue the next time I see her. Wait, that doesn't sound right. Shit, I don't even remember what we talked about or anything else for that matter. She must really like me if we spent the whole night together, he thought. Emmet smiled to himself as he approached the bar.

"I'm gonna need a hair of the dog, if you don't mind. My head's pounding like the blacksmith's working on it. Any chance you could make that evil man stop playing the piano?"

"Well, sir, I reckon he needs the practice so, no, I won't stop him. As far as a drink goes, I'll pour you one. Right after you square with your bill from last night."

"What do I owe?"

"Les see, three shots of bar whiskey at five cents each, one bottle of top-shelf whiskey for fifty cents and one week's lodging for Betty Sue for fourteen dollar. That brings it to fourteen dollar, sixty-five cent. I'll throw in this morning's chug if you pay in full right now."

Emmett fell back a step and said, "I can't pay that right now. Hell, I can't pay that until the end of the month. That's when I get paid."

"Look here, mister, if you can't afford things you shouldn't be running up a tab. That's called stealing."

Emmett, in a state of panic, reached in his pocket to see how much he had. "I can give you all I have on me -- fifty cents. Like I said, I'm good for the rest if you're willing to wait a bit. You've seen me here before. I live in town so you know I won't be running."

"Yeah, I recognize you. But that doesn't mean anything to me. You owe me the money and if you don't pay up right now I'm getting Sheriff Moore over here."

"Don't do that. Take the fifty cents now and I'll pay the whole bill later. I mean as soon as I get paid. Come on, mister. Ask Betty Sue; she'll vouch for me."

Johnny pondered for a bit. He figured he squeezed an extra fifty cents out, and that added to the extra he'd added onto the room rent gave him a tidy profit of seven dollars and fifty cents.

"Okay, Emmett. We have a deal. But know this: If you don't honor your debt with me, things will not go well for you. See that door in the corner over there? Inside is a man who's gonna pay you a visit come payment time. If you don't have the money, he'll make you pay another way. And I guarantee you will not like it. You follow?"

Emmett looked at the door as it slowly squeaked

open. A small, wrinkle-faced man with the thickest glasses he ever saw emerged from the room. His white hair was disheveled and he walked with a limp. His black eyes looked huge behind the thick glass. The frail-looking man had a huge knife, its bone handle protruding from a blood-stained sheath, on his belt. Emmett could see there was a ledger book under one arm.

"Meet my bill collector, Smiley."

Smiley slowly lifted his bony arm, his hand out, waiting for Emmett to shake it. Emmett almost laughed as he grasped the old man's hand.

His laughter died in his throat, startled at the strength in the old timer's grip. "Pleased to make your acquaintance," the bill collector whispered as he released his hand. He set the ledger down, opening it to a blank page, and removed a pencil from behind his ear. Emmett turned to Johnny, and asked, "Why does he whisper?"

"Never asked him. Never heard him not whisper. Just tell him what he needs to know, then be on your way."

Smiley entered into the ledger Emmett's name and address, the amount owed and when the payment was due. He wrote in huge, oversized block print. Then he asked Emmett to sign the bottom of the page.

"Why do I need to sign? We all know I owe the money. I ain't gonna cheat you."

Smiley glared at him with cold, black eyes and whispered, "You need to agree to the terms of the loan."

"I don't recollect seeing any terms."

Smiley turned the big, dusty book so Emmett could see where he was pointing. "It's all right there, in the fine print."

Emmett saw what looked like a smear on the paper. The writing was so small there was no way he could read it. He doubted anyone else could either.

Smiley handed him the pencil, pointing at the page. It was then Emmet saw Smiley's hand was missing a finger. He sighed as he signed his name, wondering how he got mixed up in this. The old man snapped the ledger shut, put the pencil back on his perch behind his ear and limped away.

Johnny asked, "So when will you have the money you owe me?"

"I'll have it for you in two days. No problem."

"Remember what will happen if you don't. Smiley will pay you a visit, and you won't feel like laughing when he's done. His accounting is all he lives for. Takes it very seriously. You don't want to upset him or you'll find out how much he loves to use that huge knife he carries."

"Yes, I got it. Pay up on time or Smiley will make me pay in other ways."

"That's right."

"By the way. I noticed he's missing a finger. Who did that to him?"

"He did it to himself when he found he'd made an accounting error."

Emmet vowed to never return to the saloon after he made good on his debt, not even if Betty Sue begged him.

He couldn't leave the saloon fast enough, knocking over a chair as he left for the sheriff's office. When he arrived there, he burst through the door, causing the sheriff to jump up with his gun drawn.

"Easy, sheriff. No trouble here," he shouted, holding both hands out before him. "I have an urgent message for you from Judge Hathaway."

"Good way to get yourself shot, barging in here like that. Why didn't you just come in normal like most folks do?"

"Wanted to deliver this as soon as I got into town. I rode all the way from Dry Creek, where the Judge is." He handed the sheriff the note.

"That horse out in front of the saloon the one you rode in on?"

"Yes, sir. That's Mabel. She's a good horse. Real gentle."

"Thought I saw that horse tied to the hitching post at the saloon. All night. That true?"

"You must be mistaking my Mabel for another. I just now arrived, straight in from Dry Creek, like I said."

Emmett hated lying to him. He was more afraid the Judge would find out that he didn't deliver the message until the following day. Might be cause to not pay him the money he'd promised.

"That horse ain't even breathing hard. But I guess I got to believe what you're telling me. You can leave now that you delivered it."

"Sure thing, sheriff. Make sure you tell Judge Hathaway I delivered it just as soon as I arrived."

The door closed and Moore opened the message. He read it and then cussed.

"Jesus Almighty, now I gotta find Mason and lock him up before the Judge gets back. I hate this Godforsaken job."

He grabbed his hat, handcuffs and a shotgun. Tom Moore went out the door to find his prisoner and return him to his cell.

CHAPTER FIFTEEN

Chase and Maggie walked straight to the bank, avoiding as many townsfolk as they could. Once inside, she turned to him and asked, "What am I supposed to be doing in here? The bank is usually closed today, it being Sunday."

"Just start looking everywhere for that claim. If there is one, it's either here or at the house. The man who threatened you will find you, I'm sure of that. If he catches you still hunting for it, it might buy us an extra minute or two to find out as much as we can about him."

"What do you mean, 'we?' You're going to be hiding. I'll be the one dealing with him. What if he gets too close and puts another bag over my head? I'd be as helpless as before, even though you're here. I don't think I can do this."

As Maggie spoke, her shoulders sagged and she started to tremble. Chase wrapped his arms around her. He looked down into her green eyes, suddenly realizing how pretty she was. He didn't have much experience with women, but he did know that holding her felt good. She seemed to melt right into him. They stood together like that until her shaking stopped.

Then Chase stepped back and said, "I know it's not easy to confront someone, especially if they hurt or scared you. You have my word that I won't let anything happen to you. Just let him know how scared you are. He might lower his guard and tell us something he shouldn't. He gets too close to you, I'll put him down."

Hearing Chase say those words helped calm Maggie, but not as much as when he held her. She felt safe in his arms. Like nothing could ever hurt her. She wanted to stay there, but knew they had a job to do. Now she was eager for her attacker to come into the bank. With Chase here, she knew no harm would befall her.

"That's reassuring, Mr. Mason. Thank you. Let's get in position to trap this scum who thinks he can bully a woman."

Chase shook his head. What a confusing woman Maggie was. One second she was in his arms shaking, the next she's talking as if they were conducting a business deal. He just didn't understand.

"Right, let's get to it. I think you should stay in your office. Remember, when he comes in, get him talking. Ask him all the questions you have. If he doesn't give any answers, I'll grab him from behind and tie him up until he does."

Maggie nodded and went into her office. She started to search the room. Chase watched her for a moment and then looked around the bank for a good hiding place. He finally decided to crouch behind a privacy partition next to the office. He would be able to hear everything that was said. Though he couldn't see into Maggie's office, he felt confident he could move in quickly when the time came.

Maggie had torn the office half apart, with books, papers and ledgers strewn all over the place. She had really worked to find that claim, even taking pictures off the wall to look behind them. As the sun set, she lighted the lamps around the office. She was sitting at her father's desk, looking in every drawer and cubby hole, when she heard a quiet footstep. She looked up to see the man she was supposed to meet at the creek standing in the office doorway.

"You were supposed to meet me at sundown," he hissed. "Now I'm gonna have to hurt you bad, just like I said."

"How did you get in? I locked the door."

"No need to worry about that. I have my ways. Where's that claim? You'd better have it. If you do, I'm still gonna hurt you 'cause I said I would. If you don't, I will kill you and then find it myself."

"What's your name? I don't recognize you from town."

"I ain't from town. Where is the claim?"

"How did you know about the mine? If it's your mine, why don't you have the claim already?"

"Last time, woman. Where is that damn claim?" He started slowly walking toward her.

Maggie started to cry, then sobbed,

"I'm sorry. I can't find it. My father must have put it somewhere he knew I would never look. You can see I've searched everywhere for it."

"Girl, you just made the biggest mistake of your life. Playing me like I'm some lump of dumb ass."

Before he could take another step, Chase appeared behind him like a ghost. He jammed a money bag over the man's head, spun him around and punched him in the stomach so hard he fell to the floor like a sack of flour. Chase leaned down, removed the man's gun belt and kicked it away.

Maggie sat at the desk, unable to move. She never saw anyone move that fast before. The bastard didn't have a chance. She stood up to go to Chase, but her legs were wobbly, so she sat back down.

"Well, what do we do now?" she asked meekly. Maggie felt as though she was in some kind of dream, one that might turn into a nightmare.

"We tie him up and get some answers from him."

"What if he doesn't talk?"

"Don't worry, he will. Is there any rope around here?"

"No, but we have some rawhide strips to tie the bank bags. Will they work?"

"Yep. Bring them here so I can tie his hands. Then we get down to business."

The tone of his voice, along with the look on his face, had changed.

Maggie got the rawhide strips and handed them to Chase. He turned the man over and quickly laced his hands together, then his feet. He left him on the floor with the bag still over his head.

"Okay, mister. I'm going to ask you questions. Nod if you can hear me."

The man nodded.

"What's your name?"

"Ed Grimes."

"Who told you about the claim for a gold mine being at this bank, Ed?"

When no answer came from the man, Chase kicked him. The sound of a rib bone

breaking filled the room. The man let out a moan, but didn't answer. Chase picked up a chair and smashed it across the man's chest.

"Stop, stop. I'll tell you," he screamed. "Take the bag off my head. I can't breathe. And give me a second to catch my breath, would ya?"

Chase removed the bag, staring at the man's face. It was not one he recognized. He had a narrow face with beady brown eyes, thinning black hair. One front tooth was missing.

"I'm still waiting for that name, Ed."

"I met a guy at the saloon a few nights back. Said his name was Jax. We got to drinking and he mentioned he was doing a job for someone and could use some help. All I had to do was scare the woman at the bank into giving me that claim. Said he would pay me plenty once I brought it to him. I didn't mean no harm to the lady. I just needed that money real bad."

"Once you have the claim, what are you supposed to do with it?"

"I'm supposed to go to the saloon and tell the bartender I need to talk to Jax. Then I go to the stable and wait until Jax comes with a sack of money. If I don't have the claim, I tell the bartender that I don't need to talk to Jax. That means I need more time to find it."

"Sounds like the barkeep is working with Jax."

"He is. I seen the two of them talking before I signed up for this."

"Why the stable? Why not meet him at the saloon?"

"He said he didn't want nobody seeing or hearing anything about the claim or the mine."

"Well, I got to say that's some plan. Too bad for you there will be no big payday. In fact, your plan to steal a claim is going to cost you."

"I ain't got no money, mister. Search me and find out for yourself. I got nothin' to give you."

"You have your life."

"You ain't gonna kill me, are you?"

"Not if you do as I tell you. I want you to go over to the saloon and do everything you're supposed to. I'll be following you so don't try anything stupid. I want to talk to Jax, is all. You get him to the stable, then you're free to go. You do this and you live. Otherwise, I'll kill you right here, right now."

"I'll do it, mister. Untie me and I'm on my way to the saloon."

Chase removed the rawhide and helped Ed to his feet.

"Here, you should be wearing this. It wouldn't look right if you weren't."

Maggie couldn't believe Chase was handing him the gun belt. Ed buckled it on, turned to her and said, "Sorry for what I put you through, lady."

Chase said, "Make sure you tell the barman you have the claim, then go to the stable. If you mess this up, you'll be dead before sunrise."

Ed didn't say a word, but nodded his head with a defeated look on his face. He limped out the door in considerable pain and headed for the saloon.

Maggie looked at Chase as if were a two-headed cow.

"What just happened?" she asked.

"You saw what happened. You need to get to the sheriff's and wait there until I come for you. I need to get to the stable so I can meet up with

this Jax fellow."

"This is all happening too fast. Shouldn't you get the sheriff to help you?"

"That would take too long. I have to go now. I'll see you after this is done."

Chase left the bank, closing the door quietly behind him. Ed would do as he was told, so Chase felt no need to follow him. He couldn't wait to meet the man who stole his guns. The man who'd sent someone to threaten a woman so he could steal a mine claim after her father had been murdered. This woman, who stirred feelings in him he'd never experienced. He vowed to protect Maggie with his life if need be and to punish Jax, Ed or anyone else who meant to harm her. Then he could work to clear his own name and leave Split Rock without a posse on his trail.

CHAPTER SIXTEEN

Chase made his way to the stable without being seen. The big door was closed, so he used the smaller side door. Ben was so occupied feeding the horses he didn't hear Chase come in. When he turned and noticed him, he dropped the pitchfork and practically ran to the man's side.

"I didn't know where you went when you left earlier. You left so fast I was worried something bad happened."

"Sorry, kid. I had to move quick before a friend became a dead friend. Things are good now, so don't worry anymore."

Ben had no idea what Chase was talking about. All he wanted to do now was show him the cleaned bridle. He took it from the peg and proudly held it up for

Chase to inspect. "Look how clean it is now. I spent an hour cleaning it and an hour polishing it."

Chase took the bridle from Ben and hung it from the peg.

"That's great, kid. Thanks. I need you to go hide up in the hayloft now. Do not make a sound no matter what you see or hear. Some bad men are coming here and I don't want you to get hurt."

Ben's disappointment showed clearly on his face. All his hard work didn't mean a thing to the man. He hung his head and said quietly, "I should just go home. It's getting late and my ma will be worried."

"Yes, you should. But there is no time. Hurry and climb up there. Remember, not a sound."

The boy reluctantly did as he was told, climbing the wooden ladder to the hayloft. He moved a bale of hay close to the opening and hid behind it. Chase went over to see Rebel. The horse nickered and pushed his head against his shoulder. Chase took in the smell and feel of his horse, longing for the trail. "Don't worry, Rebel. Won't be much longer before we're together again. Then we can go where we want, do what we want. Sound good to you, boy?"

The horse moved his head as if to nod, which brought a rare smile to Chase's face.

Ed painfully made his way to the saloon. As he

went through the swinging doors, he looked among the patrons for Jax but didn't see him. Going up to the bar, he told the bartender that he needed to see Jax.

"I'll let him know if I see him. Where can he find you?"

"He knows where. Now gimme a bottle of whiskey and put it on his tab."

Ed groaned as he reached for the bottle.

"What happened to you?"

"Ran right into the hitching post as I came in. Didn't even see it."

Walking out of the saloon with his whiskey, Ed didn't care that Jax would be angry when he learned he didn't have the claim. Maybe the man who kicked him knew where the claim was and wanted a sack of money too. He looked around but didn't see anyone following him. Maybe the man had his gun pointed at him right now, just waiting to pull the trigger. He felt the hair on the back of his neck tingle. Yep, he was out there all right, he could sense it. There was no choice but to go back to the stable and wait for Jax to show up. When he did, it would be two against one.

Ed muttered out loud to himself, "Yep, I like them odds. Make the bastard pay for what he did to me."

He was not afraid anymore now that he had sorted

things out. He went into the stable, still limping, and made his way to where the tall, rangy man stood.

"Any problems?"

"Nope. Don't know when, but he will show up here. He wants that claim real bad."

"Sit down where I can see you. I'm going to be out of sight over here. You stay there and wait. When he gets here, and comes close enough, I'll come out."

"Whatever you say, mister. You're the boss now."

Ed sat down and immediately opened the liquor bottle. Bringing it to his mouth, he took a long pull, then another. He felt the whiskey warming his belly, and it gave him confidence to face what was to come. The stable became very quiet as the two men waited in silence. The only sounds were the swishing of the horses' tails and the occasional stamping of their hoofs.

After Ed left the bar, the bartender, Johnny, went in the back to find Jax. He was sitting in the office drinking a whiskey, his feet up on the desk.

"I don't think the boss would appreciate you taking over his office. You come into town for a few days and think you're the mayor or something."

"If I wanted to hear from you, I'd ask. Did you hear me ask?"

"No."

"Then keep what you're thinking to yourself."

Jax removed his gun from the holster and spun the cylinder. It made a soft clicking as it went around.

"I haven't fired this in a while. Maybe you want to give me a reason?"

"Nope. Just speaking my mind, is all."

"Don't. Why did you come back here? Did Grimes finally show up?"

"Yep. Said he needed to talk to you. Didn't say where you could find him, though."

"Anything else?"

"He put a bottle of whiskey on your tab and left. Don't worry, I gave him the cheap stuff."

After a long silence, Johnny turned to return to the bar.

As he did, Jax holstered his gun, then said, "Next time you give someone a bottle, make sure it's on your tab, not mine."

What a piece of donkey shit, Johnny thought as he went out front. He only tolerated the man because he was ordered to by his employer. He couldn't wait for Jax to leave town -- and hopefully never come back.

Jax removed his tobacco pouch and rolled a cigarette. Lighting it with a stick match that he lit with his thumbnail, he inhaled deeply. As he blew out the smoke, he was already counting the money he would get when he handed over the claim. Then he could leave this nothing town and never look back.

He finished his smoke and threw the remains on the floor, stamping it out as he left the office. Jax had not left the saloon since fleecing Ben for those guns two days ago. He'd stayed in the back, sleeping during the day and fooling around with the whores at night.

He left the saloon now for the stable, keeping in the shadows as best he could. When he got there, he took a look inside and saw Ed sitting with his back against a wooden post, slugging whiskey from the bottle Johnny had given him. He wanted to be sure Ed was alone, so he leaned against the rough-sawn boards of the barn and waited. If someone was in there with Ed, Jax knew he would either spot him or Ed would start talking to him. Once Ed started drinking, he couldn't keep his mouth shut.

CHAPTER SEVENTEEN

Sheriff Moore stepped out of his office, adjusted his hat and made sure his badge was pinned on straight. He needed to look official, especially bringing in a murder suspect. He checked the 12-gauge, making sure both barrels were loaded. Getting Chase back in the cell was going to be difficult.

Maybe I should deputize a couple of men from the saloon to help me, he thought.

The saloon was crowded, everyone talking loud to be heard over the piano. He glanced around, not seeing anyone capable enough to make a difference. Most of the men were already well into the coffin varnish, and the rest weren't far behind.

"Damn it, I'm on my own, I guess," he muttered. "Someday I want to be the one throwing whiskey back, sitting in the saloon without a care in my head. Let someone else carry the load for a change."

The sheriff left the saloon, hopelessness enveloping him. Chase didn't kill Owen, but the Judge said he did. Once Hathaway returned to Split Rock, there would be a quick trial that would end with Chase swinging in the wind with a sign around his neck. All the sheriff could do now was get the drifter back in his cell, using any means he could. His job was on the line now. The Judge expected him to go along with everything that he said, whether he knew it to be legal or not. After all, it was the Judge that made certain he'd been hired on as sheriff years ago. It was made plain at the time that the new recruit was to follow the Judge's orders. Chase Mason would be just another victim of Judge Henry G. Hathaway's justice.

He started toward the other end of town where he and Chase had gone separate ways after the shootout.

It was then he saw Emmett Blackman sitting in a chair in front of the mercantile.

Emmet might be a good man to help me. The Judge hired him to deliver a message, so he might be agreeable to more work and money, the sheriff thought.

The sheriff crossed the street, walking briskly toward Emmett. When he got close enough, he asked,

"Hey, Emmett. You wanna make some extra money? It would be working for the Judge."

"Doing what?"

"Helping me bring a criminal to jail."

Emmett had been out of town when the drifter arrived, so Moore was certain that he knew nothing about Chase Mason being accused of murder.

"Sounds dangerous. But I do like the sound of extra money. How much you talking?"

"I don't rightly know. Be up to the Judge when he gets back. I'm sure he'll be very grateful."

"There gonna be any gunplay? I don't feel like dying tonight for anyone, including the Judge."

"Nope, no gunplay. You in?"

"Yep, count me in. When you need me?"

"Right now, Emmett. Let's go."

Emmett couldn't believe his good fortune. Just when he needed more money to square his debt at the saloon the sheriff shows up and wants to hire him.

Must be my lucky night, he said to himself. "Where we headed?" he asked the sheriff.

"The other end of town. We're looking for a fellow named Mason, Chase Mason."

"Well then, what's he look like?"

Sheriff Moore gave him a description. He also let

him know that Chase was armed but not dangerous. But he still handed Emmett the shotgun.

“Whoa! You said no gunplay.”

“There won’t be any. All you got to do is stand beside me and hold that 12-gauge like you mean business.”

“Okay. I can do that.”

CHAPTER EIGHTEEN

The Judge woke in a furious mood. He hadn't slept well and he could smell the thunder pot from across the room. He had been looking forward to a big breakfast, but he wasn't so sure he could eat now.

"I thought I told that woman to open the window when she left," he grumbled. "Wait until I find her. She won't forget my orders next time."

He opened his battered travel trunk and surveyed the contents, looking for comfortable clothes for the long ride back to Split Rock. Past experience taught him that wearing a suit would cause major discomfort. He would change into proper clothes once he arrived in town. He dressed in canvas pants and a wool shirt, then headed downstairs to the dining room. He decided to have breakfast despite the foul stench lingering in his nose. It would be late getting back and he might not get a chance to eat again until the following day.

"Millie, bring me a pot of coffee and some food," he bellowed. He paid no mind to the other patrons in the room.

Millie had been watching for him to enter the dining room because she knew he needed to be served immediately. She quickly put together a heaping plate of biscuits and gravy with four slices of bacon. She walked to his table with the plate in one hand and a fresh pot of coffee in the other. She placed the food in front of him and filled his coffee cup.

"Good morning, Judge Hathaway. I trust you slept well and woke refreshed and ready for your long ride home."

"No, I didn't sleep well and I'm not refreshed, thanks to you. I told you to open the window after you brought me my nightcap. I woke to the stench of the chamber pot. Even my clothes smell of it. I want you to go up to my room and empty that thing right now."

Millie was thoroughly enjoying his displeasure. He did order her to open the window last night, but she chose not to. Anything she could do to get back at him for his bad behavior, she did.

"Yes, your honor. I'll take care of that right now."

"Not yet. Leave that coffee pot and bring me something sweet, like a pie or cake. I don't want you serving me after you clean that foul thing. You're so stupid, you might forget to wash your hands after."

Instead of allowing him to see how upset she was, she replied, "I have some fresh-baked pies I just know you'll enjoy. They were supposed to be for the couple in room six. They're expecting friends to join them for the evening meal."

"I don't give a damn about that. Just get me some pie, keep your mouth shut and go clean my room. I'm used to much better service than this. I'll be speaking directly to your employer before I depart for home."

"Yes, Mr. Hathaway."

As she left for the kitchen, she heard him mutter, "It's Judge Hathaway, you imbecile."

It took all she had to stop herself from running to his room, grabbing the waste pot and dumping it on him while he ate. She was not going to let him get to her. Instead, she gathered both pies, spit on the crusts and brought them to his table.

"What took so long? Never mind, don't answer. I like you better when your mouth isn't moving."

Millie watched the fat man cut into the pie and start eating, then left. The dining hall was mostly full, so cleaning his room would have to wait. One of the girls didn't come to work this morning, so the inn was short on help.

I'll clean it myself. I don't want him here any longer than necessary. The sooner he's gone, the better, she thought. Walking to the kitchen, she noticed one of the Judge's men standing by the side door.

"Can I help you?" Millie asked.

"Excuse me, I was wondering if I could get a bite to eat for my friend and me. We work for Judge Hathaway, but he doesn't let us eat in the same room with him. Any chance you could rustle up a little something we could eat outside?"

"What's your name?"

"Name is Reese. And I'm sorry to bother you."

"I'm Millie. I can fix up a plate for you. Just be sure and bring it back."

"Yes, ma'am, I'll be sure to return it."

Millie fixed a plate of fresh cornbread muffins and beans for them. She poured some coffee in a cup then said, "I only have one extra cup. You'll have to share."

"No matter, Wade don't like coffee no ways."

Reese took the plate and coffee near the Judge's coach to eat. As he left, Millie tried to understand how someone could work for someone like the Judge. She went about her work, cleaning plates and pots, and peeling potatoes. She was busy preparing the noon meal when Reese returned with the empty plate and cup.

"Thanks, Millie. That sure hit the spot. In fact, it was so good that I didn't even share it with my partner. That coffee is some of the best I've tasted. How much I owe you?"

"You don't owe me anything. I'll just put it on the Judge's tab.

He won't even know that he bought you breakfast." She smiled as she said it, and so did he.

The Judge finished off two slices of pie, one from each pan, then sat back in his chair.

He said to himself, "I detest that woman, but damn, she can cook. Everything she makes is delicious."

Before he left the table, he pushed what remained of both pies to the floor, making sure to step on them as he left the dining room.

So much for your little dinner party tonight, he thought.

He left a trail of pie filling and crust as he made his way outside to his coach.

He wanted to check on Reese and Wade. Sometimes they took too long getting things ready and he had to remind them who they worked for.

Both men were sitting down, watching the farrier

shoe the horse. "What the hell are you men doing? I told you I am behind with my court schedule and need to leave as soon as possible."

Reese, the more talkative of the two, replied, "Just waiting for the horse to be ready, is all. The man is almost done, as you can see."

"I don't need to see anything except you two idiots loading my belongings."

"Everything is on the coach but your travel trunk. It's not packed yet. That nice Millie is going to let us know when we can get it."

The Judge was now fully enraged. He stamped his feet, waved his arms over his head and screamed, "Get your asses up to my room and retrieve my trunk. Throw my belongings in it and get it on that coach or you'll both be looking for new employment."

The two men jumped up to do his bidding. Neither liked the Judge, but they did enjoy the easy money. All they needed to do was get him from one place to another on time.

When they opened the door to the Judge's room, Millie was inside cleaning up. She was just closing the trunk as they entered.

"I was just about to come down to let you know the trunk was ready. I hope I didn't cause you any trouble, but I was very busy this morning."

Reese lied to her when he said, "No trouble at all, Millie. We'll just grab the trunk and be on our way. The Judge is waiting, so we'd better hurry. By the way, what's that smell?"

"That's the Judge's chamber pot. I haven't had time to clean it yet."

"Well, good luck with that," Reese replied.

He handed her the room key before he and Wade lifted the trunk and left the room. Millie immediately sat down and wiped her brow with a kitchen rag. They almost caught her putting some of the Judge's own shit from the chamber pot in the bottom of his trunk. She smeared it all over the sides so he would smell it but not immediately see it when he opened the lid.

I wish I could be there when he opens it, she thought. She knew it was a terrible thing to do, but that man deserved it.

Millie finished cleaning and returned to the kitchen to scrub her hands before finishing the food for lunch. She was not hungry at all but knew her guests would be. She prided herself on her cooking and wanted to please all who stayed at her inn. She glanced out the window as she went about her duties. The trunk was on the top of the coach and Reese was busy tying it down. The Judge was yelling at the man shoeing the horse, gesturing wildly with his arms. The other horses in the team ignored the commotion, but the horse that needed the shoe was nervously stamping its hooves and jerking its head. The horse reared up, knocking the farrier down and surprising Wade, who was holding the reins. He managed to calm the horse, but the Judge had jumped back, tripping and falling on his side. He roared to his feet, his coat dirty and his pants torn.

"What the hell have you done?" He screamed at the farrier. "This is your fault. You will pay for my new clothes and a bottle of good whiskey. I'm going to need a drink before traveling to set my mood right."

The farrier got up and replied, "Look here, Mr. Fancy Pants, that horse did what he done 'cause you were yelling and waving your hands about. You spooked him. My own clothes are ruined and I'm lucky I didn't get stomped on. I ain't gonna pay you anything. In fact, you owe me for my work, seeing as I'm all done."

The Judge went rigid.

"Wade, this man is charged with attempted murder of an elected official. Put him in the coach for immediate trial. Make sure he's secured properly so he can't escape. Reese, get that damn trunk down. I need to change my clothes."

Millie was enjoying the scene, especially when the

Judge fell down. She didn't mind that the Judge tore his trousers when he stumbled. Her enjoyment ended abruptly when she noticed Reese getting the trunk down. It wouldn't take the judge long to figure out what the foul smell in his trunk was and who had put it there.

Millie ran to the dining hall, looking desperately for any one of the other girls working at the inn. She needed to find someone quickly to take over the kitchen so she could hide from Judge Hathaway. She ran through the inn, looking for help. She finally saw Anna bringing in water from the well.

"Anna! Thank God I found you. I need you to take over the kitchen duties right now," Millie practically yelled.

"All right, but you look scared. What's wrong?" Anna asked.

"Never mind that now. All you need to know is, if anyone asks for me you haven't seen me."

"I don't like to lie like that. So if I'm asked anything, I will tell the truth. I can work in the kitchen for you, but you'll have to finish bringing in the water for me."

"Anna, I'm sorry. I should never have asked you to lie for me. It's just that I might have done something to really anger Judge Hathaway. He's very upset and there's no telling what he'll do to me."

"What do you mean, 'might have done?' You either did or didn't do something. Is he mad at just you or everyone who works here?"

"Pretty sure he'll be mad at everyone he sees. Won't matter if they work here or not."

"I'm not going anywhere until you tell me what you did." Anna folded her arms and looked at Millie sternly.

"I put some shit from the thunder mug in the Judge's clothes trunk. He tore his trousers when he fell outside. Now he's coming back to his room to change into clothes that will stink to high heaven. He's likely to kick my guts out."

"Oh Millie! I don't care for that man either, but you should never have opened his trunk in the first place. You can't involve me in this. He'd likely have both us bull whipped.."

Millie's heart sank. Anna was right, asking for her help had been wrong. This was something she needed to deal with on her own.

"I'm so sorry I asked you to help me. This is my mess. Never mind going to the kitchen. I'll go back, do my work and wait to see what happens next.

Thank you for being honest with me."

"You're welcome," Anna replied as she picked up the buckets and went about her business.

Millie returned to the kitchen, unsure of what to expect from the Judge, but knowing she wouldn't like it. She was putting wood in the cook stove when she heard the Judge yell, "Get that trunk up to my room right now. I'll be up after a few drinks from the bar to settle my nerves."

"Yes sir, I'll take it there as soon as I get the room key from Millie." Reese found Millie at the stove.

"Millie, I hate to bother you but the Judge needs to return to his room. He fell and ruint his clothes, so he wants to change. Do you still have the key?"

"I do. I've been so busy I haven't had time to return the key to the office. I'll go up with you. Just let me take this pot of stew off the stove. It has to cool a bit."

She followed the men carrying the trunk to the Judge's room and unlocked the door. Wade and Reese put the trunk on the floor while Millie opened the windows. The room still reeked of the chamber pot's contents.

"Let's go back outside, Reese. It stinks in here, and we should check on the horse, anyway." Wade said.

"Yep. Let's go. Don't need to watch him dress. I'm sure he'll come down when he's ready to get going."

Both men left and Millie was alone in the room.

She was terrified but needed to come up with some kind of excuse to tell the Judge when he discovered his clothes were ruined.

She heard boot steps on the stairs and panicked. Millie did the only thing she could think of. She opened the trunk and grabbed the chamber pot. She threw its contents over his clothes as he walked through the door.

"What in God's name is that foul smell?" the Judge bellowed.

"I'm so sorry, your honor. I don't know how it happened."

"How what happened, you stupid girl?"

"I'm so clumsy I dropped the waste pot. I must have tripped over something. I can't believe it myself, but it fell right into your opened trunk."

After she said it, she started crying. Holding her hands over her face, she turned from him. She was afraid to face his anger.

"Stop crying like a baby, you stupid fool. Get that damn pot out right now and then clean my clothes. You can keep the trunk. I'll get a new one and put it on your tab. Now I have to stay an extra night, so I'll need another room. Can't sleep in that stench. . On the house, of course. And free drinks at the bar. And keep out of my sight for the rest of my stay, lest I sentence you for being so clumsy."

Any other time, the Judge would have really punished her. But he was exhausted from the earlier incident with the horse and a poor night's sleep.

I'll get even with her the next time I overnight here, he thought.

"Of course, Judge. Right away. I'm awful sorry."

When she turned to face him, he had already left the room. She couldn't stop shaking the whole time she spent getting the smelly clothes out. "I will never do something like this again," she said to herself. She set the clothes in a tub of water to soak while she cleaned the trunk. "At least he thinks it was an accident."

Millie inspected the Judge's new room and found it satisfactory. She placed a bottle of the inn's best whiskey on the nightstand. Even though all his expenses for the extra night would be paid by her, she didn't mind. She thought it a small price to pay, given what could have happened.

When Millie gave Reese the room key for the Judge, he smiled and said, "I sure thought you were in big trouble when I heard what happened. How come he didn't charge you with a crime?"

"I really have no idea. I was expecting much worse.

Maybe he was having such a bad day that he couldn't handle any more."

"It was a bad day for sure. Just ask the farrier. He's chained in the coach, awaiting the trial."

"What trial? All he did was shoe a horse."

"The Judge seems to think it was attempted murder of an elected official."

"How can that be? All I saw from the kitchen window was the horse rearing up and knocking Judge Hathaway down."

"Judge claims the farrier spooked the horse so as to trample him to death."

"Oh that poor man. What's going to happen to him?"

"All depends on the Judge and his verdict, I guess. Wade and I saw the whole thing, but we won't go against Henry. We need a paycheck and the work is easy."

"Well, then, I guess I'm the only other witness. You think I should be at the trial? When is it?"

"First thing in the morning, right before we head back to Split Rock. As for you being there, it's not for me to decide, Millie."

"Do you think the farrier actually planned to have the horse kill the Judge?"

"I'm steering clear of answering that. I've got a lot of work to do. Take care, Millie."

Reese walked away without looking back. Millie wanted to help the poor man in chains tomorrow, but didn't know anything about the law. She would be taking a big risk if she did.

She was going to have to sleep on it. Maybe she'd know what to do when she woke.

CHAPTER NINETEEN

The Sheriff and Emmett walked to the very edge of town, looking everywhere for the drifter. Peering in windows and leaning around corners, they themselves looked suspicious.

"I don't know where else to look for the man. I'm starting to think he left town," Emmett said.

"If he did, he would want his horse. Let's head over to the stable and see if his horse is there. If he is, then he's still in town," the sheriff said. The two headed to the stable, their boots kicking up puffs of dust as they walked. As they got closer to the stable, they could see light through the windows. The sheriff told Emmett to be careful.

"You stay here and cover me. I want to look in the

window before we go inside. I want to know what we're walking into."

"All right, sheriff. I'll stay put and keep an eye out."

The sheriff made his way slowly to the window. He saw a man he didn't recognize sitting on a bale of hay. He was taking long pulls from a whiskey bottle. There was no sign of Ben, and that worried him. Why would a stranger be in there drinking alone? He was about to head around to the door when he noticed a slight movement in the shadows. He didn't see anything else move, but noticed that Rebel was still in his stall. As he watched the horse, it was paying no attention at all to the stranger on the hay bale. Every other horse had its head or ears turned toward the man sitting on the bale. A horse like Rebel would be watching his every move, ready to bite or kick if he came too close. That was when the sheriff realized that Chase must be in the barn as well. That would explain Rebel not even looking at the man, content knowing Chase was nearby.

Sheriff Moore moved very slowly away from the window and crept toward Emmett.

"Jesus, sheriff, you look like you seen the Devil or something."

"Chase is in there and so is a man I have never seen before."

"So what? Let's go in there and get your man. If the other causes any trouble, arrest him too."

"It ain't that simple, Emmett. That man I'm after is up to something and I aim to find out what it is."

AS MAGGIE MADE her way to the sheriff's office, she saw him talking to Emmett at the edge of town. She stopped, waiting for them to finish and head back to the office. To her surprise, they turned and started off to the opposite end of town.

The sheriff wasn't one to walk around town at night unless he had a clear purpose, which made Maggie wonder what they were up to. She followed the two men, careful to stay far behind them. She watched as they slowly searched around the outskirts of town. They stopped briefly and talked, then headed in the direction of the stable, walking a little faster, as if they'd figured something out. She followed and watched as the sheriff looked in the stable window and then whispered to Emmett.

Apparently neither the sheriff nor Emmett had realized they were being watched by Maggie. When she suddenly appeared out of the darkness, both men jumped.

"What the hell are you doing? Sneaking around in the dark like that. We could have shot you."

"Looks to me you might have missed, the way you jumped and all," Maggie replied.

"This is official business, so you need to leave right now, Maggie," the sheriff said.

"I'm supposed to be over at the jail with you, so I'm safe."

"Who told you to go there?"

"Chase did. He's trying to arrange a meeting with the man who hired Ed to threaten me."

"Wait, who's Ed?"

"He's the man who came looking for the deed to the mine. Apparently he's just a hired hand. Someone else is behind all this business about the mine and Chase is going to help me figure out who it is."

"You have no idea who hired this Ed?" the sheriff asked.

Maggie shook her head. "That's what Chase is trying to find out. All we know is that his name is Jax."

"What's Ed look like?"

As Maggie described Ed, the sheriff's eyes flicked to the stable window. The man she described was sitting on the hay bale. The sheriff realized what Chase was up to. He was inside the barn, using Ed as bait.

Somehow Chase knew the man who'd hired Ed would show up at the stable if Ed was there.

"All right. Now that I know what's what we are going to stay out of sight and wait to see what happens in there."

Maggie's gaze drifted to the stable window. "Who is in the stable, Ben?"

"Nope. Your Ed is in there."

"Shouldn't you get Chase? He was using this fellow to get to Jax."

"No need to. Chase is in there, too, hiding somewhere. Who knows what will happen after Jax shows up." The sheriff shook his head. He didn't know whether he was angry at Chase or himself. *How does the man figure all this out? He knows more about what's happening in town than I do,* the sheriff thought.

Emmet cut in, his voice jittery. "Hey, sheriff, this is starting to sound like this here shotgun won't be enough. I think I'll head back to my place and get my rifle."

"You stay put, Emmett Young. You ain't goin' anywhere right now. You said you wanted in and now you're in."

"How about more shells for the shotgun?"

"Sorry, didn't bring any. Like I said, all you got to

do is look like you will shoot. Now, let's see your mean face."

Emmett made the meanest face he could and Maggie had to stifle a laugh. He didn't look mean at all, but the sheriff said, "Jesus, you look as mean as a pissed off rattlesnake. You're gonna do just fine. Anything happens, make that face and point that shotgun. That will stop anyone in their tracks for sure."

The sheriff's words made Emmet feel much better. He really didn't want to shoot anybody, so if he could stop them with his mean face -- all the better.

CHASE WATCHED Ed drinking on the hay bale. He had seen so many other men just like him. Drifting from town to town, no job, no money, no real purpose. Sooner or later they all ended up either dead or behind bars. Chase knew the same fate was in store for the man who had attacked Maggie. One way or another, he would pay for what he did to her. Chase's thoughts were cut short when Ed stood up and drunkenly shouted, "I need to go outside for a spell 'cause I got to piss, mister. I mean right now, cause I been holdin' it awhile. This here whiskey done run right through me."

Chase thought about it before he answered. There was no telling what time Jax would show up.

If Ed was outside when he arrived Jax might not come into the stable. So Ed would have to relieve himself inside the barn. "Sorry, Ed. I can't let you go outside. If Jax sees you he might not come inside. Go over to the first stall and do what you need to in there. If it's good enough for a horse, it's good enough for you."

"Damn it, mister. I ain't no animal. Why can't I just wander outside to do it? I ain't gonna stand behind a horse and let go."

"Then you can piss yourself, for all I care. You have two choices. Pick one."

JAX WAS ABOUT to go in the barn to get the claim when Ed stood up and started yelling. At first he thought he was just talking to himself. When he heard a second voice he knew Ed wasn't alone and he stopped in his tracks.

Who the hell is in there with him? Maybe that stupid boy, Ben. He stepped back in the shadows by the door, not wanting to go in until he knew who it was. Maybe Ed was trying to set him up and take the claim for himself. Jax wasn't about to let that happen.

Jax's plan was to plug Ed full of holes once he handed over the claim. He didn't want any loose ends walking around, especially with the way Ed ran his mouth when he drank. He'd probably have to kill the boy, too. He didn't know if the kid would figure out what was going on, but it was better to be safe than sorry. No one cared about that boy anyway.

He watched quietly as Ed walked into one of the stalls. It looked like he relieved himself, then slowly made his way back to the bale of hay, sat down and started drinking again. Jax didn't see or hear anyone else in the barn, but knew Ed wasn't alone. He would have to sneak in and get the jump on whoever was with Ed, or get Ed outside somehow. If it was a trap, whoever was in there would have to follow Ed. Then Jax could kill them both and get the hell out of town with the rights to the mine. He bent low and started looking for anything he could throw at Ed to get his attention. He heard voices coming from the side of the stable.

Someone else was here? A sense of urgency flooded through Jax. He needed to get that damn claim from Ed before he gave it to someone else.

Jax went in the barn as quick as he could, moving

quietly to the outside wall. He made his way to the tack wall and stopped to listen. The only sound was Ed burping and mumbling something about not being an animal. Jax crawled across to where Ed sat and slowly stood up, out of sight from where he figured the other person was hiding. Ed was so far into the bottle that he didn't even realize Jax was there until he whispered, "Give me the claim, Ed, or die right here." As he said it, he held his finger to his lips, telling Ed to be quiet. As he reached his hand toward Ed to get the claim, he felt the pressure of a gun barrel against his skull.

"Throw your gun belt on the ground right now or keep it and see what happens next. I don't much care, either way. You choose."

Jax knew the man had the drop on him, so he removed the gun belt, letting it fall to the barn floor. "You're making a big mistake, mister. Best you mind your own business and leave me to mine."

"I am minding my own business."

"What I ever done to you? I don't even know you."

Chase ignored him, turning to Ed, who was now so drunk he could barely sit upright. "You can go now. Best you leave town and don't ever think about hurting a woman again."

"Geez, mister, I wouldn't never hurt a woman and I

ain't got no plans to stay in this town." Ed stumbled as he got up, knocking over the empty whiskey bottle, then lurched his way to the barn door. He walked right into the sheriff and his posse as they came around the corner.

"Hold it right there. You're not going anywhere just yet," the sheriff said. "Maggie, find something in here to tie his hands. I only got one pair of handcuffs. Emmett, keep that scatter gun on him 'til we know why he's here."

"Okay, sheriff. Let me know if you want me to fill him full of holes. I kinda want to hear this thing go off."

The sheriff looked at Emmett, not believing his ears. "Just keep him covered, is all. Besides, you said you didn't want any gunplay."

"That was before I turned mean." He made his mean face to show the sheriff he meant what he said. The sheriff turned away, almost laughing as he did. His voice was cold when he commanded, "Chase, put down the gun and raise your hands. Step away from the other guy."

"Sheriff, I don't think you know what's going on here. Leave me be so I can take care of this my way," Chase said.

"You're right. I don't know. But I do know you're

gonna do as I say or so help me God I'll shoot you here and now. All I want to do is bring you back to my office and sort this out."

"We can do that right here, Tom. No need to go anywhere."

"Well, Chase, that's where you're wrong. The Judge is due back in town tomorrow and he expects you to be in a jail cell, awaiting trial. My job is on the line and I don't want to lose it."

"I see. So you're not an elected official, you're someone appointed by a corrupt judge, having to jump to his orders."

"Bottom line is I'm bringing you in tonight."

"What about this jackass?" Chase pointed to Jax.

"We'll bring him in too, if that makes you more agreeable."

"That's the only way I'll go with you. Before we go, I need Ben to identify this man to make sure he's who I think he is."

"I'm not gonna wait around while someone goes to find Ben."

"No need to look for him, he's up in the loft right now."

"What the hell is he doing there?" the sheriff asked.

"I'll explain later." Chase glanced up at the loft. "Ben, you can come down now."

Everyone looked up at the muffled steps, and then one boot at a time appeared on the ladder rungs. Ben made his way down and walked over to the group, keeping his distance from Jax.

Chase looked at Ben then asked, "Is that the man you paid to clean my guns?"

Ben looked at Jax, then quickly turned away. He was so frightened all he could do was nod.

"Ok, sheriff. Let's all go to your office." Chase glanced at Maggie, then frowned at the sheriff. "By the way, I told Maggie to go to your office and stay there. What is she doing here?"

"She just showed up. I told her to leave, but she wouldn't. I don't want anyone to see you walking around packing pistols when you're supposed to be in jail. Unstrap that gun belt and hand it over."

As Chase slowly removed his gun belt, the sheriff handed him the handcuffs. "Put these cuffs on, Chase."

Chase put one on his left wrist and one on Jax's right, then said to him, "You're gonna pay for the things you've done in Split Rock."

"I ain't done nothin' I wasn't told to, so you got no right to threaten me. Right, sheriff?"

The sheriff didn't answer him. He put Chase's gun belt over his shoulder, then ordered the three men to start walking to the sheriff's office. "Maggie, go home now. You'll be safe seeing as I have these men in custody."

"What about Chase? He didn't do anything wrong. Why are you doing this?"

"Just go home, Maggie. This no longer concerns you. That goes for you too, Ben."

Maggie turned to Chase and asked, "What should I do?"

"Do what the sheriff said. Ben, go home. I'm sure your ma is worried. Maggie, you go home, too. Look for something to keep you busy until I get to the bottom of this. And remember, no good deed goes unpunished." As he said it, he gestured with his head as though he was trying to tell her something.

Ben did as he was told. Maggie looked at Chase and said, "I'll check on you tomorrow. Maybe bring you something to eat if I have time to make it. I'm sure I'll be very busy at the bank seeing as it's Monday."

"Thanks, Maggie. See you then."

As the group of men passed the saloon they heard the piano playing and the raucous noise of the patrons enjoying themselves. Every man in the group wanted to stop and have a drink.

Emmett put the shotgun in the corner of the sheriff's office and left for home. Moore removed the cuffs from Chase and Jax, then untied Ed's hands. The sheriff opened one cell door and gestured for Chase to go in. When he did, the Sheriff locked the cell door right away. Chase wasn't expecting that and it angered him. He was even more upset when Jax and Ed were not put in the other cell. Jax sat on the edge of the sheriff's desk as Ed hunched over, retching in his hat.

"What the hell is going on here?" Chase asked. "Why aren't those two in a cell?"

Sheriff Moore ignored him. He told Jax to take Ed outside so he could get some fresh air, maybe sober up a little. He watched as they walked directly to the saloon.

The sheriff shook his head and said, "Look here, Chase, I tried to do the right thing but that's not gonna work now. With the Judge coming back tomorrow there's no more time for you to find Owen's murderer. If you are innocent, and I think you are, the Judge will see to it that you go free."

The sheriff couldn't even look at Chase when he said the last part. The trial would find Chase guilty and the Judge would sentence him to hang. It didn't sit well with him, but there was nothing he could do now.

Chase grabbed the cell bars and shook them

violently. “If you know what’s good for you, you’ll get me out of here. This is all bullshit and you know it.”

The sheriff acted as if he didn’t hear a word. He got up from his desk and walked out the door, heading to the saloon for a much-needed drink.

CHAPTER TWENTY

Millie slept fitfully through the night. When she finally decided to get up, it was still dark outside.

She had no idea what to do about the trial. The farrier was innocent and the Judge corrupt. If she involved herself, there was no guarantee that it would help the accused man.

The Judge hated her and might even charge her with something. Millie decided to go to the kitchen and start a pot of coffee. She was completely at home in the kitchen and enjoyed starting the day there. Lighting the wood stove, she decided to cook some bacon to go along with her morning coffee. As she sat by the window, she sipped her coffee and ate the delicious bacon. She saw the coach where the trial would be held. Though it was warm in the room, she shivered, thinking of the fate of the poor farrier. It was then she decided to try to help him.

Millie made sure that a good breakfast would be available to all her guests, even though her mind was racing on something else. She knew the Judge liked his morning meal and she didn't want to anger him before the trial started. A plate of fresh eggs, bacon and hot cakes would surely have him in good spirits. She even baked his favorite, apple muffins, to accompany him on his journey back to Split Rock. Soon after deciding to cook him the best meal she could, he arrived in the dining hall, bellowing for food and drink. Millie prepared his meal and had to stop herself from adding any foul ingredients as she normally did.

As she placed the plate in front of him, he asked, "What took you so long, you lazy cow?"

Millie fought the urge to dump the whole pot of hot coffee on him. Instead, she filled his cup and replied pleasantly, "I went outside to get fresh eggs for you. That's why it took a little longer."

"Well, I hope they taste as good as they smell. I'm starving."

"Let me know if you need anything else, your honor."

Millie left the table, thinking her plan to make him happy this morning was working.

Judge Hathaway consumed his morning meal without really tasting the delicious food. His thoughts were on two immediate concerns: the trial of the farrier and getting back to Split Rock.

As he sipped the last of his coffee, he looked out at his coach, replaying the events of yesterday. The more he remembered, the more convinced he was that the man awaiting trial in his courthouse was guilty. Whether he sentenced him to hang immediately or punished him in a lesser manner was not important. He had to return to Split Rock as soon as possible to resolve the murder of Owen Montgomery. The Judge pushed his cup away and scraped the wooden floor with his chair as he stood.

He saw his coachman walking by the kitchen and bellowed, "Reese, get what's left of my belongings loaded on the coach. Don't let that idiot girl touch anything, I won't tolerate another incident."

"Right away, Judge. I'll take care of it."

"I want to leave as soon as the trial is over this morning. I'm already days late for my next case."

"I understand, your honor. Wade and I will do our best to get you where you need to be as fast as we can."

"I expect as much. Now go get my things, get them loaded and wait for my command. I'm not sure what the verdict for this trial will be, so stay alert. Have the hanging rope at the ready in case we need it. I don't want to waste any time trying to find it. Every minute counts from now until we reach our destination."

"Yes, sir. As you say."

The Judge walked by the kitchen on his way outside. When he looked in, he saw Millie at work, preparing breakfast plates for other guests. He stopped and proclaimed, "Don't think I've forgotten what you did to my things. I'll be sure to take care of you the next time I stop here. I'm certain it won't be long, you stupid, stupid girl."

He turned and waddled out the door without a backward glance. Millie stood by the stove, watching him as he made his way to the coach. He had no idea she was going to be a witness at the trial.

She brought the food to the dining room and returned to the kitchen. After wiping her hands on her apron, she removed it. *No sense wearing an apron to a trial,* she thought.

Leaving the warm kitchen, she went outside, carrying the apple muffins she had baked for the Judge. Millie hoped they would influence the man to be forgiving toward the farrier. The closer she got to the coach, the more her hands trembled. She came to a stop by the fancy door and knocked, barely able to breathe.

"This court is about to be in session. I cannot be bothered at this time, so go away."

Reese and Wade were in position in the driver's seat, ready to be off as soon as the trial was over. Reese watched Millie, a look on his face as if he couldn't believe what he was seeing. Millie knocked again, this time saying, "I am a witness in this trial."

The Judge replied, "What makes you think you can be a witness?"

"I saw the whole thing happen from the window."

Judge Hathaway was not surprised someone had seen the event. He was, however, surprised someone would have the gall to take part in his trial. The farrier didn't know what to think, judging by the shocked look on his face.

"Please come in and let me welcome you to my courtroom," the Judge said.

The door slowly swung open. The Judge curious to see who dared enter his courtroom. When he saw Millie, he was relieved. He knew she would have no influence on his verdict, no matter what she said. He was, however, upset that her involvement would slow the proceedings.

"You can sit there, next to the defendant."

Millie noticed the soft cushioned seat the Judge had as she tried to make herself comfortable on the unforgiving plank seat she shared with the farrier. She had never been so frightened in her life.

"Welcome to the courtroom of Judge Henry G. Hathaway. We are here to determine the guilt or innocence of the defendant. Please state your name for the court, sir."

"My name is Will Tuttle."

The Judge removed a small bible from his vest pocket and held it up. "Will Tuttle, do you swear to tell the truth and nothing but the truth, so help you God?"

"Yes sir. I ain't never lied yet and I ain't about to."

"Will Tuttle, you have been charged with the attempted murder of an elected official. How do you plead, sir?"

"I didn't do nuthin'."

"The court did not ask you if you did anything. It asked how you plead?"

"Like I said, I didn't do nuthin'. I been chained up since yesterday and forced to sleep in this here circus wagon with no food or water."

Millie dared to speak. "Will, you can have an apple muffin after this is over."

"Mr. Tuttle. This court now finds you in contempt.

If you do not plead either guilty or innocent, the court will determine your plea for you."

"Is there a plea in the middle of guilty or innocent? I ain't gonna plead guilty, that's for sure. But maybe I could have held that horse a wee bit better. Not sure of that neither, me being old and all."

"No, there is not. You can be only guilty or innocent. Which is it?"

"If I plead guilty, what happens to me?"

"The court decides the punishment, depending on testimony heard."

"If I plead innocent?"

"The court decides the verdict, depending on testimony heard."

Millie spoke again. "I would like to speak on behalf of Mr. Tuttle."

Judge Hathaway turned to her with hatred in his eyes. "Are you his lawyer, miss?"

"No, your honor. I'm just someone who witnessed what happened that day."

"Well, because you are not Mr. Tuttle's lawyer, you cannot speak on his behalf. You can, however, testify as a witness. Tell the court your name."

"My name is Millie Johnson."

The Judge removed the small Bible from his vest pocket again and held it up. "Millie Johnson, do you swear to tell the truth and nothing but the truth, so help you God?"

"Yes, I do."

"The court asks Millie Johnson to recall the events of yesterday in regard to this trial. That is specifically what she claims to have seen during the attempted murder, of an elected official."

"I don't think Will would do such a thing. He's a good, honest man, who works hard every day for his family."

"Miss Johnson, the court does not give a tinker's damn about what you think of Mr. Tuttle's work ethic. It does, however, care about the truth. Please tell the court exactly what you saw and only what you saw that day."

Millie was now more nervous than ever. She had planned to say all good things about Will.

Now all she could do was try to remember how the accident had happened. Both Will and the Judge looked at her intently as she retold the events as she saw them, leaving nothing out.

"Is that all, Miss Johnson?"

"It is."

"Mr. Tuttle, you've heard the witness. Do you have anything to add to her testimony?"

"Nope. That is what happened all right."

"Mr. Tuttle. How do you plead, sir? Guilty or innocent?"

"Well, sir, it appears that Millie and I both think I didn't do nuthin' wrong. So I plead not guilty. That means it's two against you, don't it? Looks like I'm a free man again. I wanna thank you so much, Millie."

Millie smiled and patted Will on his shoulder. She was proud of herself for having the courage to take part in the trial. She handed him a muffin, which he ate quickly. Her whole body jumped when the Judge rapped the gavel against the side of the coach.

"The court has heard the testimony of both the defendant, Will Tuttle, and the witness, Millie Johnson. This has been a unique trial in that the judge presiding is also the victim seeking justice. Therefore, for the charge of contempt of court, the judge finds the defendant not guilty."

Both Will and Millie couldn't believe their ears. Not being guilty of contempt of court might mean not guilty of the other, more serious charge. They leaned as far forward as they could as the Judge spoke again.

"As to the charge of attempted murder of an elected official, the court hereby finds the defendant, Will Tuttle, guilty as charged. The punishment for this crime shall be death by hanging, to be carried out immediately following this trial."

Will and Millie sat in stunned silence. Neither could understand how a trial like this, let alone a death sentence, could even take place. Unable to breathe, Millie left the coach to get some air as Reese climbed down from the seat with a rope with a noose on one end.

"For the love of God, can't you stop this?" she pleaded to Reese.

"I don't like it neither, but I can't interfere. I would lose my job, and I don't want that to happen."

"That man in the coach is going to lose his life and he doesn't want that to happen either. Which is more important, Reese?"

As Reese turned away, Millie threw the muffins at him. "I never want to see you at my inn again. You, Wade and Hathaway will not be shown any courtesy from me as long as I live. You can all go to Hell."

Millie could barely walk the short distance back to the inn on her own. Crying and shaking, she sat in the kitchen. She lifted her head, looking outside when she heard Will screaming for someone to help him. Reese was attaching the rope to a post off the back of the coach and Wade was slipping the noose around Will's neck as he stood on a wooden milk pail. The Judge came out of the coach, holding a black cloth bag, which he handed to Wade.

"Mr. Tuttle, a word before we proceed. The court may reduce your sentence if you know anything about a Ned Mason or Matt Ballam."

"I ain't no friend of neither. What do you mean, if I know something?"

Will's voice became muffled when the bag was forced over his head. All Millie heard were his screams as she watched in horror. "Somebody help me. I didn't do nuthin'."

The Judge held his arm up for a second, then dropped it. Wade kicked the pail out from under Will's worn boots, leaving him to swing gently in the slight breeze until his arms and legs stopped twitching. Reese lowered the body and removed the rope, coiling it neatly.

"What should we do with the body?" Reese asked.

"Leave it for Millie to take care of. She wanted to be involved, and now she is. She needs to learn that there are consequences for every decision you make. I see her watching from the kitchen."

Wade opened the coach door for the Judge. As he stepped up, he turned and waved to Millie, a big smile on his face.

"That should teach these people not to interfere with me," he said to Wade.

The stagecoach left the inn in a cloud of dust,

heading for Split Rock, as the Judge yelled to the driver, “Don’t spare the horses. We can buy more.”

Judge Hathaway settled in his cushioned seat, feeling satisfied with the results of the trial.

The court would hand down a guilty verdict to all who attempted the murder of an elected official. He smiled to himself as he remembered the look on Millie’s face as he rendered the verdict. Seeing that look was almost as enjoyable as watching the guilty man hang. He had a feeling she would never again involve herself with the dealings of his court. The Judge made a mental note to get that woman fired the next time his coach stopped for an overnight there.

CHAPTER TWENTY-ONE

Sheriff Moore couldn't get to the saloon fast enough. He needed whiskey to wash down the ugly taste in his mouth after what he'd said to Chase. He couldn't stand the position he was forced into and wanted to tear off his badge and drop it into the nearest spittoon.

At the bar, he told Johnny to fetch him a glass and a bottle. It was going to take several drinks to make him feel right again. He noticed Jax and Ed sitting at a table in the corner, so he made his way over and joined them. He practically broke the whiskey bottle when he slammed it down on the table. Twisting out the cork, he filled the glass to the top and drank it in one gulp.

"Jesus, Sheriff. What's got you all lathered up?" Ed asked.

The sheriff didn't say a word. He poured himself another drink and emptied the glass.

"You gonna share that or drink it all yourself?" Jax asked.

"It ain't for you two idiots, that's for sure. If I had half a brain working, I'd arrest the both of you and throw away the key. But I can't do that, can I? Judge Hathaway will be back in town tomorrow. Without that claim to give him, there's going to be hell to pay. You'd better find it before he arrives."

"It's all Ed's fault, Tom. He had plenty of time to get it. The Judge can take his anger out on him. Nuthin' to do with me, so I ain't worried."

"You'd better be worried, you fool. You're the one who hired Ed to threaten Maggie. The Judge is going to want to know why you didn't do it yourself, seeing as you're on his payroll."

"Listen up, sheriff, and listen good. I don't give a damn who you think is to blame. I ain't working for you, so shut your pie hole and mind your own business. You have plenty to ponder. Judge Hathaway will be wanting to know where your prisoner is." Jax stood abruptly and left the table, knocking his chair over as he did.

Ed sat looking at the sheriff, a confused look on his face. "What's happening? Am I still gettin' paid? I worked real hard trying to get that claim for Jax. It ain't right me not gettin' paid, is it, sheriff?"

"That's between you and Jax. Now leave me alone so I can drink in peace."

"I ain't happy about this. I don't cotton to people cheating me out of what's coming to me."

"I agree with you, Ed. Go tell that to Jax. He's at the bar right now, talking to Johnny."

Ed turned to look, seeing Jax and Johnny laughing together, looking right at him.

"One thing makes me madder than a fox without a hen is someone laughing at me. I ain't gonna stand for it," he said to Sheriff Moore.

As Ed left the table, the sheriff poured himself another glass. This time he sipped it, as he tipped his chair back against the scarred wall to see what happened next.

With any luck, they'll kill each other, saving me all kinds of trouble, he thought.

JAX LEANED against the bar as Ed came toward him. Something about the menacing look on the man's narrow face made him wary. "Get that pepper box ready, Johnny. Ed means business."

The bartender reached down to make sure the gun was there. Ed walked right up to Jax and stood eye to eye with him. "Exactly what's got your mouth so twisted anyway?"

"Nuthin' to do with you, Ed. Step away now like a good boy before someone gets hurt."

"I'll be leaving when I'm done talking to you. And I ain't done yet. Where's my pay for what I done for you?"

"Well, you didn't do what I asked, so I reckon I don't owe you anything."

"Maybe not, but I sure did spend some time trying. That's gotta be worth something."

"Well, Ed, you're right, it is worth something." He asked the barkeep for a bottle of cheap whiskey. "Here you go. One bottle of the best whiskey this saloon has, in payment for the hard work you done for me."

Ed looked at the bottle sitting on the bar, his mouth watering. "I'm thinking two bottles is what is owed. I ain't leaving without another to keep that one company." He stood, one hand on his gun, waiting for Jax to say something.

Jax wanted to shoot him in the face for asking for more. "Looks like we need another bottle, Johnny." The barkeep placed a second bottle on the bar. Ed smiled a crooked smile as he reached for the bottles.

"Nice doin' business with you, Jax. I reckon we be square now." The two whiskey bottles clinked together as Ed turned and walked away.

Sheriff Moore watched Ed as he left, surprised Jax had let him go. He thought Jax would keep him close, to use him for his excuse to the Judge for not finding the claim. *Oh well, not my problem. I got my own shit to worry about.* He poured another whiskey, letting the front legs of his chair down to the floor.

CHAPTER TWENTY-TWO

Maggie continued on the way to her home. What had Chase been trying to tell her? He'd said "keep busy and no good deed … ." That's it! He wanted her to keep looking for the claim. It made the most sense. She needed to get home and find it even if it took all night. And it if wasn't at home, she'd go to the bank early and look for it there again.

IT HAD to be hidden in a place where father could get to it but where no one else would look for it, she thought. She walked briskly toward home, determination on her face. She was the only one who Chase could depend on, and she did not want to let him down.

. . .

SHE SEARCHED THE HOUSE, methodically, starting in her father's office. After several hours, she was exhausted, frustrated and hungry. It was clear the claim was not in the house. She felt like crying as she sat at the kitchen table. Now she would have to go back to the bank and continue searching. The whole thing was a mystery. She knew the deed had something to do with her father's death, but what? And would finding it help find the killer? And why was Chase in jail when the sheriff clearly thought he was innocent?

UNABLE TO FIND the strength to go upstairs, Maggie fell asleep at the table. When she woke, her whole body was stiff and sore. She stood up, stretching, and rinsed her face with water as she thought about what she should do. Before she decided, her stomach rumbled, letting her know it was time to eat something.

I'LL MAKE breakfast and bring some over to Chase. He'll know what to do.

. . .

THE SMELL OF EGGS, bacon, potatoes, biscuits and coffee filled the room as she cooked. She went in to the pantry, bringing out a small picnic basket, and carefully placed the food and utensils inside. No longer tired, she headed to see Chase, picnic basket in one hand and coffee pot in the other.

SHE REACHED the sheriff's office and kicked the door with her small boot. When no one opened it, she put the food and coffee pot on the rickety bench by the door. She pushed the door open to find Chase standing in his cell looking at her. The sheriff was nowhere to be seen.

"DID YOU FIND THE CLAIM?" he asked immediately.

"No, but I did bring you something." Maggie went back out and came in with the food and coffee.

"THAT SMELLS GOOD. I haven't eaten in quite a while."

MAGGIE OPENED the small square door on the cell

and passed Chase a plate, followed by a cup of coffee. He was so hungry he didn't even wait for her to get her own serving. He devoured three eggs, six slices of bacon, a huge pile of potatoes and two biscuits before she was able to sit at the sheriff's desk. "I guess I don't have to ask if it was good. Let me get you more coffee to help wash down that food."

AS SHE HANDED him the coffee, their fingers touched briefly. She liked the way it felt. Her fingers so delicate and his so rough and strong. She sighed, then returned to the desk to eat her breakfast. "I spent all night searching the house for that claim. I'm certain it is not there. I'm going back to the bank as soon as I leave here. Maybe I overlooked something the other day."

"SOUNDS LIKE A GOOD IDEA." Chase sipped the coffee. "Even though you didn't find what we're looking for, I do feel better. That food was just what I needed and the coffee is the best I ever tasted. When I make it, I can never get it right. It's either way too strong or way too weak. You'll have to show me how, sometime, after all this is over."

. . .

MAGGIE like the idea of showing the big, tough drifter how to make good coffee. In fact, she liked the thought of her showing him much more. She blushed and turned from his gaze before he saw how he was affecting her.

"SINCE THE SHERIFF isn't here, can you look for the keys to the cell? When he left last night I didn't see him take them," Chase said.

MAGGIE PUT her cup down and rummaged around the top of the desk. She opened each drawer,

but the keys were nowhere to be found. She pounded her fist on the desk in frustration, hearing a jingle of metal. Looking under the desk, she spotted the key ring hanging on the side of the drawer. She smiled as she held them up for Chase to see.

MAGGIE FUMBLED with the key until the cell door lock clicked. She ran in to the cell and threw her arms around Chase, his body feeling like chiseled rock to her. She felt so safe in his arms that she didn't want to leave. Chase enjoyed the softness of her against him briefly before saying, “Maggie, we have to go before the sheriff gets back. Get your things and let’s get going.”

SHE PUT THE PLATES, utensils and cups back in the basket and grabbed the coffee pot while Chase strapped on his guns.

MAGGIE HELD UP THE BASKET. “I need to bring these home to clean them, and you need to freshen up. You smell like a horse that was rode hard and put away wet.”

CHASE SMILED AT THE COMMENT, then said, “There’s no time for any of that. We need to get to the bank and locate that claim. It has to be the connection between Owen and his killer.”

THEY LEFT the sheriff’s office for the bank.

MAGGIE GLANCED UNEASILY toward the bank. “What

if Sheriff Moore or someone else sees you? You're supposed to be in jail."

"DOESN'T MATTER at this point. I'm running out of time to clear myself. I tried to work with the sheriff, but he's not interested in finding the real killer. All he wants is me in the cell when that judge returns so he doesn't lose his job. If anyone tries to stop me, I can't let them. Just keep walking if someone does. I don't want you getting hurt."

HEARING Chase say that made Maggie feel good. He wanted to protect her even though she'd shot at him days ago. She wanted to stop and hug him again, but didn't dare to. Instead she replied, "Something smells here, and I don't mean you. Well, I mean, you do smell, but not that way. Why did the sheriff let both Ed and that Jax go last night? He should have locked them up."

BEFORE CHASE COULD ANSWER HER, he saw the sheriff coming out of the saloon. He grabbed Maggie's arm and pushed her along. “Keep going. I’ll meet you at the bank later.”

MAGGIE TURNED TO CHASE, about to ask him why, when she spotted the sheriff approaching them. She locked eyes with Chase, nodded, and kept walking. At the bank, she locked the door behind her. She found the “Closed” sign and placed it in the window. She began her new search of the bank.

CHAPTER TWENTY-THREE

Sheriff Moore couldn't believe it when his blurry eyes saw Chase and Maggie together. His head hurt from too much whiskey and too little sleep. The last thing he could remember was watching Ed leave the saloon with two bottles of whiskey the night before. Then it hit him: The Judge was returning today and Chase had to be back in jail. He watched as Chase stopped and Maggie went in to the bank.

"Hold it right there, Mason. I guess little Miss Maggie found the keys and let you out. That so?"

He wobbled slightly as he waited for Chase to answer.

"That's right, sheriff. You sure are good at figuring things out. Too bad you can't figure out who killed Owen."

"I don't need to do anything of the kind. All I need to do is put you back in that cell, where you belong. Then I'll arrest Maggie for helping you escape."

"Sheriff, if you know what's good for you you'll keep on walking and forget you saw me."

"The Judge says you're guilty and your trial will prove it. I'm bringing you back to the cell."

"You're drunk and look like you haven't slept in a while. Even on your best day you couldn't bring me in. In case your bloodshot eyes didn't notice, I have my two best friends with me this morning." Chase patted the pistol handles affectionately with each hand, his eyes hard and his body ready.

The sheriff knew the stranger was right. There was no way he was going to take Chase in alone, especially today. He was just about to turn and leave when the swinging doors to the saloon opened and Jax and Ed came out. They quickly made their way over and stood beside the sheriff.

"Well, well. What be happening here, sheriff? Looks like you might need some help," Jax said.

"I reckon so. He broke out of jail and doesn't want to go back."

Chase studied the three men and still liked his odds. If he had to, he would shoot Jax first, then the sheriff. He figured Ed would bolt at the first shot. If he didn't, Chase would send a bullet his way.

"Ed, I told you to leave town," Chase said. "Offer still stands. Leave now and I won't shoot you. Or stay and … , Your choice."

Ed looked at Chase, standing there confidently, then at the Sheriff and Jax. They looked nervous and unsure. He made his decision quickly. "I ain't no part of this and I don't want a bullet in me." He turned and almost ran from the men facing each other.

"Looks like you're down a man. That Ed's a smart one for a dumbass. He knows when to leave. Either of you smart like Ed?"

Both the sheriff and Jax stood their ground. Ed had run back into the saloon and now a knot of people were standing outside, watching the three men.

"Looks like it's gonna be just us. Make your move, sheriff. Remember, I asked you to walk away."

Sheriff Moore stared at Chase, realizing he had no chance against him. He looked to Jax, almost not recognizing him. His face was contorted and his eyes wild, like a cornered, crazed animal. He knew then that Jax was going to pull his gun on the drifter.

He slowly turned back to face Chase, his hand on the butt of his holstered gun. He shuffled his feet in the dirt for better balance and tried to remain calm. He was visibly shaking.

The stranger looked like a coiled rattlesnake, ready to strike. The sheriff was about to call it off when Jax made his move. He tried to draw his pistol, but it never cleared the holster.

The drifter's bullet tore through his gun hand, forcing him to let go of the pistol. He screamed in pain and fell to his knees, shouting at the sheriff to shoot.

Chase had holstered his gun, even though the sheriff's remained pointing at him.

"Go on, sheriff. Try your luck, like your friend, Jax, there. I'll even use my left hand so you have a chance. By the way, what hand do you use to pin that badge on in the morning?"

"I use my right. Why you askin'?"

"Just wondering, is all. We gonna stand here and bullshit all day or we gonna do some shooting?"

The crowd of people from the saloon had moved closer, eager to hear what the men were saying.

"Come on, sheriff. Put some holes in that murdering bastard. What are you waiting on?"

"Shoot, shoot, shoot!" The mob yelled.

Now the sheriff had no choice. Chase just stood there, his hat tipped low to keep his face in shadow.

The sheriff could swear the man's eyes glowed under the brim.

The sheriff thumbed the hammer back and tried to pull the trigger, but he wasn't fast enough. A gunshot split the air and a bullet slammed into him. He looked down at his arm to find it covered in blood. He watched in horror as the blood dripped, forming a small pool in the dirt. The stranger had drawn so fast the sheriff never saw the movement. He lowered his damaged arm, as the onlookers slowly backed away from the scene.

Chase walked to where Jax was still kneeling and picked up his pistol. He opened the gun, spun the cylinder and removed the bullets, which he put in his pocket.

Throwing the gun in the dirt, he went to the sheriff and did the same with his pistol. "Looks like you'll be having trouble putting that badge on for a while, Moore. Now run along, boys. Leave me to my business or I swear I'll make things worse for you."

THE SHERIFF HELPED Jax to his feet, picked up both pistols, and the two wounded men limped back to the saloon.

"How are we gonna explain this to the Judge?" Jax asked.

"Never mind him right now. Tell Betty Sue to get Doc over here and Johnny to fetch us some whiskey."

"We're in big trouble, Moore. I was supposed to have the claim by now and you were supposed to keep that drifter in jail. What's our plan now? The Judge should be here by sunset."

"Jesus, man. Give me a chance to think." The sheriff could barely catch his breath the pain in his arm was so severe. "You made things a lot worse for us when you pulled your gun on him out there. Did you really think you were faster?"

"No, but there were three of us at first. That reminds me, where is that bastard Ed? I'm gonna teach him a lesson he'll never forget. I cain't believe he run off like that."

"What did you expect? You already paid him for what he done. Why would he get in a gunfight for nuthin? I sure as hell wouldn't."

"I told him before we came out of the saloon he would get paid good money after the drifter was dead. We even shook on it. He should never have left us like that. He struck a deal and should have seen it through."

"Rightly so, but he didn't. We'll deal with him later."

The doctor came in, carrying his black medical bag. "What did you boys do now, shoot each other over a card game?"

"Something like that. Fix us up quick as you can, Doc. We got a lot of loose ends to tie up." The sheriff said.

"I'll do what I can. Looks like the bullet went clean through your arm. It tore up some muscle on the way out. I'll have to stitch some things back together. Be better doin' this in my office."

"Right here will do. Give me that whiskey bottle." The sheriff took a long pull from the bottle, and then another. "Okay, doc. Get to it."

The doctor did what he could for the sheriff's arm before turning toward Jax.

"Let's have us a look at your hand, son."

As he examined Jax's hand, the doctor whistled. "Looks like today is your lucky day. The bullet just missed a vein and all your knuckles. You'll have limited use of it for quite a while, months maybe, depending on how you treat it. Eventually, the hole will fill in, leaving a terrible scar. Meanwhile, I'll stuff some cotton in there, wrap it up good and see what happens. Hopefully it won't get infected. Come see me if the pain gets bad. I can prescribe some morphine if you need it."

"Thanks, Doc," Jax quietly said.

"You hear what he says, sheriff? It's my lucky day today. Maybe I'll find that damn claim before Judge Hathaway comes back." Jax grabbed the bottle and took a swig, wincing as he did.

"Good luck with that. If Ed couldn't scare Maggie into finding it, how you gonna find it with a lame hand? Even worse, now that drifter is in the mix."

"We just need more men. How many you think we need? I say five would do it."

The sheriff reached for the whiskey. The pain in his arm was starting to dissipate thanks to the effects of the liquor. Now it was a dull throb. "Well, we had just three and you saw how that worked out. We need at least ten hard men. Men who will kill for money. You must know some."

"I might know someone who can get the men we need. He's gonna want to see some money up front, and he won't come cheap."

"Get him to help us. I'll get the money. How soon can you ask him?"

"One more drink and I'm on my horse. I should be back in about two hours. You'd better have the cash.

These men will just as soon kill us for free if we cross them."

Sheriff Moore left the saloon, holding his arm against his side as he walked back to his office.

He said aloud, "Where the hell is Hathaway? I need him here right now to straighten this pile of shit out."

He reached the office and kicked the door shut. He needed some time to think.

CHAPTER TWENTY-FOUR

After the gunfight with Jax and the sheriff, Chase reloaded his pistols. Each bullet that he'd fired had hit where he aimed, so there was no need to find the lead. He headed to the bank to see how Maggie was coming with the search. The door was locked, so he knocked until he heard Maggie call out, "The bank is closed today. Come back tomorrow."

"It's Chase, Maggie. Let me in."

The window shade moved and Maggie looked out at him before she opened the door. He entered the bank while she closed and locked the door behind him.

'Any luck finding the claim?"

"Not yet. I heard guns. What happened?"

"Let's just say the sheriff and his sidekick challenged me in the street. Now they need to see the doctor. I shot Moore in the arm and the other in his hand. Don't worry, they'll both live."

Maggie stood next to Chase, admiring the way he looked in the dim light of the bank. His dark, whiskered face made his blue eyes even deeper. With a straight nose, square chin and broad shoulders, he was easy to look at, even if he did need a bath. She put her arms around his waist and looked up at him, waiting for a kiss. Chase wanted to kiss her, but he pushed her away and said, "Please, Maggie. We have more important things to do."

He walked away from her and asked, "Where should we start looking?"

"I already searched here, but I believe this is where he would hide it."

"Okay, then. We're not leaving here until we have that claim. Let's get started."

Maggie rolled up the rugs, looking under each one. She removed the framed paperwork from the walls and looked to see if the backing had been removed, then replaced. Chase removed all the drawers from the expansive mahogany desk, checking the contents. He even tipped the desk on its side to look underneath. Going to the large bookcase, he removed each book, turned it upside down and fanned the pages. They spent two hours scouring the room and its contents.

"Well, if it's not here, where the hell is it?" Chase asked.

"Maybe he gave it to someone like his lawyer, for safe keeping."

"What about the bank safe? That's where I would keep it."

"No. That's the last place father would keep it. Too obvious."

Maggie was exhausted, so she sat in her father's big leather chair behind the massive desk. "I can't believe we haven't found it. There is no place else to look."

Chase stood in the middle of the room. He slowly turned in a circle, looking around one last time before calling it quits. It was then he noticed the hat hanging from a hook on the wall. He slowly walked to it while Maggie hung her head and closed her eyes. He remembered the time Maria told him a story about a client who hid his folding money in his hat.

"Well, I'll be the back end of a pig. Look here, girl." Chase held the hat out toward her with one hand. In the other was a piece of folded paper.

Maggie almost fell out of the chair in her haste to study the paper.

"I found it inside, under the sweat band."

He handed her the paper, which she unfolded and

read. "It's a homestead claim with Chester Hale's name on it. It's for five- hundred acres and includes access to Stone Creek, which runs down from Bald Mountain, all the way to Cold Water Lake. But how does this claim help us find who murdered my father and clear you?"

"I don't have a clue, Maggie. But I sure as hell know it has something to do with it. We can't tell anyone we have it. He didn't even tell you, so your father hid it for good reason."

"No mention of a gold mine on it. So why was Ed talking about a claim to a gold mine?" Maggie pressed her lips together. "Oh, and there's something else. The day Ed attacked me, I asked him his name to help me find the claim. He wouldn't give me his name, but said the name on the claim was Chester Hale. This is what he wanted."

A feeling of hope surged within Chase. It was starting to come together. "I remember the sheriff telling me a man was hanged before I came to town. He stole money, then killed a man. The man he killed was Chester Hale."

"I don't know anyone by that name, but it does sound familiar. Maybe he was someone my father knew. I should have looked into that sooner."

"Listen here, Maggie. Your father was murdered,

you were attacked and threatened. With all that going on, it does not surprise me that you didn't catch that. Even if you had we would still be in the same spot we are now. We have the claim, but we don't know who is behind all this. How would having the claim benefit anyone but Chester Hale? You think of anyone he would leave his homestead and land to?"

"No."

"Seems I need to have a chat with Ed. Make sure it was Jax who put him up to attacking you. Once I find that out, we'll know more about what we're up against. Keep that claim with you. I'm going to the saloon to find Ed and get my saddlebags."

"Please be careful, Chase. I don't want anything to happen to you."

"Don't worry about that. Where will I find you later?"

"I'm going to ask the undertaker if Mr. Hale had any family. Then I'll be at my father's house."

"Meet you there after I talk with Ed."

Chase was determined to get answers from Ed. He didn't mention to Maggie that he hoped Jax was at the saloon, too. He was going to get his guns back, and it was time to make Jax pay for stealing them.

CHAPTER TWENTY-FIVE

Chase entered the saloon ready for action. Ed and Jax were nowhere to be seen. He kept the wall at his back as he made his way to the bar and motioned the barkeep over.

"You got something of mine, mister. Hand them over, nice and slow."

Johnny reached under the bar, his hand touching the pepper gun. For just a second he thought about pulling it, but didn't. He moved his hand to the saddlebags and slowly handed them to Chase, who slung them over his shoulder.

"Where will I find Ed and Jax? Don't feed me any bullshit or I'll put you on my list of things to take care of before I leave town."

"They're in the back, mister. Having a chat. Want me to bring you to the office?"

"No need. I can find my own way. Don't try to warn them. You don't want any part of this."

Johnny just nodded and continued wiping the bar. He knew Jax would be angry, but he was more afraid of this drifter.

Chase silently walked behind the bar, looking for the office. He heard voices coming from the right, so he angled that way. He noticed a door slightly opened and saw Ed sitting in a chair. He made his way to the side of the door, listening to the two men talking. It didn't take long for Chase to figure out that Ed was in trouble with Jax. He kicked the door open, going in with both guns drawn.

"Put your guns on the floor. I don't want to kill you, but I will, so just do it."

Ed practically threw his handgun to the floor and put his hands in the air. Jax stood facing Chase, his gun in his good hand and a glass of whiskey in the bandaged other. He raised the glass to his lips and downed the drink in one gulp. The empty glass shattered as it fell from his grasp.

Jax sneered at Chase as he said, "You just made a big mistake, mister. Coming here alone was not a good idea. I ain't gonna put my gun on the floor."

Before Jax could say another word, Chase put a bullet through his gun hand. Jax screamed with pain, grabbing the newly wounded hand with his bandaged one. His gun had fallen to the floor with a thud when the bullet struck.

"Looks to me like you did what I asked after all, seeing your gun is on the floor now."

"You'll pay in spades for what you done here. You wait and see, mister. You'll be swinging from a rope before sun up," Jax gritted through his pain.

"Talk is cheap, just like the whiskey you drink. Now, sit down and don't say a word unless I ask you something."

Chase picked up both handguns and unloaded them, putting the cartridges in his pocket. He threw the guns in the corner of the room and took a chair facing the door. Ed was downright scared and even Jax was visibly shaken.

"Can I get a bandage for my hand? I'm losing a lot of blood. You said you didn't want to kill us," Jax said.

"The sooner you answer my questions, the quicker you can get that hand looked at."

Chase despised both men, but he wasn't about to let them die. He wanted to put a beating on Ed for his actions against Maggie, but he had helped out at the stable. Jax deserved more punishment than a mere beating. He was responsible for hiring Ed, cheating the stable boy and stealing Chase's guns.

"Ed, is this the man who hired you to obtain the claim from Maggie?" Chase gestured toward Jax.

"Reckon I don't know what obtain means, but it be him that hired me."

"That's all I need to hear from you. Get out before I change my mind." Chase jerked his head toward the door and Ed scrambled up from the chair, wincing as he did.

"Thanks, mister. I'll be leaving town around sundown. Won't be putting eyes on this place again." Ed hurried out the door, not even stopping to pick up his pistol in the corner.

Jax glared at Chase and gritted his teeth from the pain in both his hands. "I need to see the doc. I can't stand the pain any longer."

"You ain't seeing anyone until you tell me where my guns are."

"Those were your guns I took from that dumb kid?"

"He's a kid, but not dumb. Just too young to spot a liar. Now where are they? I'm not asking again."

Jax regretted his earlier decision of not leaving the saloon to get the hired guns. Instead, he'd noticed Ed coming into the saloon and had decided to bring him in the back room to rough him up. He wanted to make Ed pay for running away from the gunfight. Now he was trapped here, wounded, with no one to back him up. Not even Johnny, who had surely heard the gunshot, had come to help. He was alone. Maybe if he told the drifter where his guns were he'd let him go, like he'd done with Ed.

"Your guns are in Smiley's room."

"You mean upstairs, where the ladies are?"

"At the end of the bar, in the corner. That door leads to Smiley's room."

"Who is this Smiley fella?" Chase asked.

"He keeps track of the money for Johnny. And he makes sure the people who owe pay on time."

Chase reached down and grabbed Jax by the front of his shirt, yanking him to his feet. "Let's go."

They left the small office, went down the back hallway and into the saloon. "Get me my guns." Chase growled.

Jax knocked on Smiley's door and then entered without waiting to be let in. Smiley sat at a small desk in the corner, the black ledger book open before him. Chase looked at him, not sure what to think. He had expected a younger man. A man people would fear.

"Smiley, would you give this man the guns I asked you to hold?" Jax asked.

The old man rose from his chair and walked to a huge safe. He opened it, reached in and turned. He held the cloth-wrapped guns in his thin arms. Chase took them from him without a word, then walked out the door, dragging Jax with him.

"You have what you came for, now let me go. I need the doc to patch me up," Jax pleaded.

"Not just yet. I need to know who's behind all this. It damn sure ain't you, I know that much. You ain't got the brains. So who is it?"

Jax didn't answer right away, so Chase reached over and grabbed the hand that was bandaged, squeezing hard. Jax practically fell to the floor in pain as he shouted, "Sheriff Moore. It's him telling me what to do. It's the sheriff."

Chase released Jax's hand. "You go see the doc now. Get yourself patched up, then put this town behind you. If I see you here tomorrow I'll put you six feet under. You follow?"

"Yeah, I got it. Could be I see you tomorrow, maybe I plant you instead." Jax was braver now that Chase had let him go.

"Good luck with that. You can't even hold a gun. Go on, get out of my sight. You make me sick."

Jax stumbled off in a rage that both his hands were useless to him. When he walked past Johnny, he sputtered, "It's all Ed's fault. If he hadn't run off that drifter would be pushing up daisies right now."

The bartender smiled as Jax lurched through the swinging doors. *Serves you right,* Johnny thought, as he poured himself a whiskey.

CHAPTER TWENTY-SIX

Jax left the saloon, heading straight for the doctor's office. He needed to get his left hand patched up and something for the pain. He burst through the door. "I been shot! My other hand's been shot."

Doc Hodges pulled his medical bag from his desk. "You sure have a nose for trouble, mister. Who keeps shooting you in the hands?"

"That drifter, the one who killed the banker. The sheriff had him locked up good but he got out somehow. I need to be on my way, so be quick about fixing my hand. Gonna ride and get some help to kill that son bitch."

"Seems more likely he's going to kill you. Why

don't you let Sheriff Moore handle this? You need to rest and give those hands time to heal."

"I can't do that. It was the sheriff told me to get more help. If I don't, we're all gonna be dead from that drifter's lead."

Doc cleaned and wrapped the wound, thinking about what Jax had said about the stranger. He had carried Maggie to his office the other day. Though he was in the sheriff's office, he hadn't been locked up then. . Doc Hodges didn't know anything about the drifter, but he did know about Jax, and Jax was trouble. He decided it was best to get the sheriff and let him deal with the whole thing. Besides, what honest man gets himself shot twice in a matter of days?

Jax moaned. "Don't you have any painkiller, Doc?"

"You rest while I get what you want."

Seeing his opportunity to render Jax unconscious so he could get Sheriff Moore, Hodges went into his office and unlocked his medicine cabinet, where he kept the laudanum. He mixed it with some alcohol and handed his patient the glass. "Drink this. It will ease the pain."

Jax took the glass and gulped down the contents. "Thanks, Doc." He tried to stand but couldn't.

The doctor pushed him gently back down into the chair. "You need to stay here for a spell. Let the medicine do what it's supposed to. Your pain will disappear soon."

"Ok, Doc," Jax murmured as he fell asleep in the chair.

The doctor left his office, heading to see the sheriff. He trusted Tom Moore a lot more than he did his patient. The sheriff was at his desk, a worried look on his face. "What's troubling you, Tom? Is it your arm? If you're in a lot of pain I can give you something for it," Doc Hodges said.

"No, Doc, it's not the arm, though it does hurt. What can I do for you?"

"I just wanted to let you know that the same man who got shot with you is in my office right now. He's been shot again. By that drifter."

"I swear if there was a stray shot fired it would find that man. He has the worst luck."

"Well, I don't think luck has anything to do with it. He's a drifter, much like that other. I don't know what he's up to, but I'm certain no good will come from it. You must have a notion of what he's doing in town. You seem to be with him enough."

The sheriff frowned. "I appreciate your concern, Doc. I really do. But you need to mind your own business, stay out of mine and let me do my job."

"I only wanted to tell you about the shooting. In case you didn't know."

"Well, now I know. Get back to your office and play doctor. Don't you have a patient over there?"

Doc Hodges didn't like the way Tom was talking to him. "Tom, you need to settle down. I'm only trying to do the right thing here."

"Leave right now before I lock you in a cell. I have things to do."

"I hope you know what you're doing, Tom. Seems to me you're on the wrong side of the fence this time." The doctor turned and walked out the door, leaving it open.

The sheriff pounded the desk, causing him to flinch with pain, which made him even more upset.

"If I could shoot with my left hand I'd kill that bastard Mason right here and now. Then I wouldn't have to worry about the Judge and his damn trial. Where the hell are those hired guns that Jax was supposed to get?"

He got up from his desk, his face flushed with anger, and headed out the open door. He slammed it shut so hard that it didn't latch and flung itself open again. He burst through the doctor's door, breathing heavy.

Doc Hodge looked up from the counter, where he

was cleaning bandages and swabs after tending to Jax. "Jesus, Tom, you don't have to come in here like that. You could have damaged my door."

"I don't care about your door. Where's the man who was here?"

The doctor was in a foul mood from the sheriff's earlier comments, and his rude entrance didn't help. His voice was mocking when he replied, "How should I know? He didn't leave a note. Why don't you go have a drink at the saloon? That's something you must be good at seeing as you're there all the time. Now get out of my office. I have real work to do."

Doc stood there, his hands on his hips, waiting for the sheriff to leave.

Sheriff Moore grabbed the doctor by his lapels and shoved him to the floor. "Don't ever talk to me like that again. I'm the sheriff of this town and you will show me some respect." The sheriff turned away and stormed out, making sure to leave the door open.

CHAPTER TWENTY-SEVEN

Chase sat at a table in the bar. He put the cloth-wrapped guns in front of him. Slowly untying the rawhide straps, he revealed the guns and inspected them closely. They were just as he had left them at the stable. He opened each to see if they were loaded and found they were. Satisfied, he called to the bartender. "I'll have a touch of your best whiskey. It's been a strange few days."

"Sure thing. I'm wondering, how did you get out of jail without a trial?"

"That's my business, not yours. I see your friendly with that Jax fella. Did you know that he stole my guns and hid them in your saloon? That makes you an accomplice."

"I don't know anything about any gun stealing.

And I damn sure ain't complicated. I'm a simple man earning a fair wage."

"I didn't say complicated, I said … ." Chase's voice trailed off. There was no way to explain what he meant. "What do you know about someone called Smiley?"

"He works for me. Does my collecting when I need him to."

"I see." Chase glanced at the door he was pretty sure Smiley was still sitting behind. He'd see about him later. He threw some coins on the bar and left.

He decided to check on Ben and get Rebel ready to ride should he need to leave town abruptly. Chase didn't see Ben when he arrived, so he went straight to Rebel and hugged him.

"Hey boy, am I glad to see you." The horse leaned against him. Chase ran his calloused hands over the horse's neck, then put his thick fingers through Rebel's coarse mane. "Won't be much longer, boy. We'll be on the trail again soon. I promise."

Rebel swished his tail as Chase threw the saddle blanket on, then hoisted the saddle into place. He cinched it down tight, then added the saddlebags and put the guns in the scabbards. He laced on his slicker and bedroll, then removed the halter, replacing it with Rebel's bridle, which the horse was eager to accept. He noticed how clean everything was, so he knew Ben had taken good care of his things. He made sure the saddle guns were properly secured before leaving the barn to check in with Maggie.

As he walked to the bank, he couldn't help but notice a huge cloud of dust coming straight toward town. Chase stopped in the middle of the street as a dirty stagecoach arrived. It stopped at the saloon, the horses lathered in sweat and gasping for air.

"No horse should be pushed like that," Chase said aloud. He watched as the two men in the driver's seat got down. One of them started to attend to the horses while the other opened the door. A plump, short man climbed out and immediately started yelling, waving his arms wildly and stamping his feet. Apparently, he wanted his travel trunk brought into the saloon, because he settled down as soon as the two men got it down and brought it in.

Chase already didn't like this man. The horses should have been cared for before the arrogant, fat man's trunk. He approached the coach and waited for the two men to return. When they did, Chase said, "Where I come from, you push horses like you did they get taken care of first. Who the hell is in charge here?"

"Well, mister, it ain't us." The tall one said. "We

just do what we're told, is all. We damn well know how to care for the horses, but Judge Hathaway demanded his belongings be brought to his room immediately. Who the hell are you anyway? Don't reckon I've seen you around here before."

Instead of answering, Chase asked, "That was the Hanging Judge?"

"The one and only. So, who are you?"

"Name's Mason, Chase Mason."

"Mason? Any kin to Ned Mason?"

Chase was stunned when he heard his father's name, but didn't show it. "Why you asking?"

"Wondering is all. We was over in Long Pine a ways back, in the saloon drinking coffin varnish. Bunch of rough-looking men come in all liquored up and lookin' for trouble. When they started abusing the whores, a local deputy tried to step in and stop them. One of the gang warned him he would end up just like the last lawman that interfered."

The man had Chase's complete attention. This might be a lead to help him find his father's killer. "Did you hear someone use my father's name?"

"No, not then. By the way, name's Reese. This other fella is Wade."

Chase shook hands. "You were saying about Ned Mason?"

"Look, Wade and I have to get the coach cleaned up and the horses put away. The Judge won't like it if he sees me talking to a stranger before our work is done."

"Understood. Let's walk and talk. I can help you with the horses; it will make for shorter work."

"Okay, let's get on with it then."

Wade went into the coach and began wiping the dust off the seats and side curtains. Reese and Chase unhitched the horses and walked them to the stable. Ben was back, and took the horses into the small corral on the side of the big barn. He pitched some hay in the feed basket and filled the trough with fresh water.

"So, Reese, why would you remember Ned's name. Who is he to you?" Chase asked.

"No one. Judge heard of him, though. He made me carve his name on the inside roof of the coach. He gets money from the governor if he hangs whoever kills a lawman. Teaches folks not to mess with lawmen and makes the governor look good."

"Why do that? Carve his name inside the coach?"

Wade shrugged. "Every time Judge Hathaway sits in it he sees the names. Every time he hangs someone he asks them if they know anything about the men."

"Why would anyone tell him if they did?"

"The Judge promises to reduce their sentence if they have good information."

"How many names you carve so far?"

"Just two. Ned Mason and Matt Ballam."

"Anyone ever say something about either man?"

"We were over in Dry Gulch for a trial, short time ago. Man robbed a general store and stole a horse. Judge Hathaway found him guilty and sentenced him to hang. Just like always, Judge asks the guilty man if he knows Ned Mason or Matt Ballam. He starts talking, and come to find out he rode with the Littlefield Gang for a spell. Left the gang years ago, right after Vernon Littlefield shot a man in the back, killing him. Said he heard the dead man's name was Mason and that he was some kind of detective."

Chase couldn't believe it. This was a major lead to his father's killer. "I happen to know a bunch of men went looking for the killer but never found him. At least now I have a name to help me find him. By the way, did the Judge reduce the man's sentence?"

Wade made a grimace and shook his head. "Nope, hung him like he always does."

Chase was more eager than ever to leave Split Rock now that he had the name of his father's killer. But first he had to clear himself of murder. He thanked Reese and left the stable to see Maggie.

CHASE STOPPED at the door of the bank and watched Maggie work. Every time he saw her a strange feeling came over him. He wanted to rush in and hold her close, feeling her body against his. He liked the way she melted into him and looked up with those beautiful green eyes. He quietly opened the door and stepped in.

"Maggie, we need to sit down and figure out what's going on here. That damn Hanging Judge is back and it won't be long before he comes for me."

Maggie couldn't help but smile when she saw him, even though he was so serious. She wanted to run to him and hold him against her, feeling his body against hers. Instead, she walked to him and said, "I agree. Let's go over everything we have so far. Maybe something will become obvious. Before I forget, I spoke to the undertaker. Chester Hale had no kin."

Maggie took the "closed" sign from the hook on the wall and hung it on the door. She locked the door, then pulled the shade. She sat at her father's desk. . Chase paced the bank, telling her everything that had happened to him since arriving in Split Rock. As he spoke, Maggie wrote it all down so they could read it afterward. Then she wrote down everything that happened to her since her father's murder.

"I'm going to read all this aloud," she said. "You listen and say the first thing that comes to mind."

As she read, Chase stared at her intensely, listening to every word. When she finished, he thought for a moment. "It sounds like I'm guilty of killing your father. But I didn't, so we must be missing something."

"The I.O.U. has to be in the middle of all this," Maggie said. "Why would my father hide it under his decanter? And what about the homestead claim? He hid that in his hat."

"And why did the Judge borrow that much money from Owen? And why wasn't it in the bank's books?" Chase asked.

"The only time we don't enter it in the ledger is when it's a short-term loan. The money would be paid back in less than a week."

"So we have the Judge borrowing money from Owen that he will pay back in a week or less. We have Owen getting killed. We have Owen hiding Chester Hale's homestead claim in his hat band. We have Chester getting killed, with no remaining family. We have the Judge hanging the man who killed Chester. We have me as a suspect in your father's murder."

"When you say it like that it seems either my father, the Judge, or both were involved in something shady having to do with this mine."

"Now, Maggie, you know your father wasn't doing anything shady. I think all this points a finger at the Judge."

"But who would be foolish enough to challenge a Judge who hangs people for the slightest offense?"

"That would be me, Maggie. There's no one else can do it. He's as guilty as the day is long.

We just need to prove it somehow."

"But how? That judge is not going to admit anything to us. Why would he? He has the last say around these parts. The sheriff couldn't stop him either, even if he wanted to."

"Sheriff Moore isn't worth the tin used to make his badge. We can't count on him to do the right thing, seeing as he takes his orders from the Judge." Chase looked at Maggie. He was reluctant to leave her but he needed to think things through. "I need to get on Rebel and ride a spell. I think better in the saddle. I promise I'll be back to see you through this."

"You'd better, Chase. I'm putting all my faith in you to find my father's killer."

"I'll be back. Keep those papers in a safe place."

"Wait a moment, please." Maggie stood up, pushed

the chair back and walked over to Chase. She tilted her head back, her green eyes wide and staring into his. "I can't think of a better place for these."

She handed him the I.O.U. and the homestead claim. Chase started to refuse them but then took them from her small, delicate hand. He tucked them under his shirt. "See you when I get back."

Chase left the bank, heading for the stable. He opened the barn door. Rebel started to stamp his hooves and shake his head. Chase led him outside and mounted up. The horse was excited to be back with his owner.

"Mr. Mason, where you going? Will you be coming back?" Ben yelled from the hayloft.

Chase waved to him, then left a cloud of dust as Rebel galloped off, leaving Ben to wonder if he would ever see the man and horse again.

CHAPTER TWENTY-EIGHT

Chase let Rebel gallop for a while, then eased him into a canter, then a walk. The soft thudding of Rebel's hooves allowed Chase to relax. He was at home in the saddle, not wanting to turn back at all.

There was no proof that he killed Owen, but there would be a warrant out for his arrest. Even so, he knew he would return to Split Rock to find the killer and clear his name. Otherwise he'd be running his whole life for something he didn't do.

He brought Rebel to a stop near a stream, where the horse could drink and Chase could think. A plan was coming together in his mind, but it would take a miracle for it to work. He touched the reins, turning Rebel back the way they came, and the horse broke into a canter, eager to return.

"You sense I'm running out of time, don't you?" Chase said to Rebel. The horse seemed to understand as he changed to a gallop.

When they got back to town, the horse slowed to a walk. He whinnied as they passed the stable, and continued on to the saloon. Chase tied Rebel to the hitching post, but didn't go inside. He removed the shotgun from its scabbard, then took the bandolier loaded with 12-gauge shells from his saddlebag. He slung the belt over his shoulder and headed for the sheriff's office.

BEN HEARD Rebel whinny and ran outside in time to see Chase stop at the saloon, take something from beside his saddlebag, then walk away. Ben felt strongly that the stranger might need his help. He hurried through his remaining chores and closed the big stable door. He ran to Rebel, let him know he was there, and stroked the horse's muzzle. "Good boy, Rebel, good boy."

The sawed off was missing from Chase's saddle, so he knew there would be trouble soon. Ben took the rifle from its scabbard and followed Chase. He wasn't sure, but thought the man was headed for the Sheriff's office. He stopped across the street and sat down to wait. No one noticed him nor the rifle he cradled.

With nothing to do but wait, Ben checked to see if the rifle was loaded. It was.

CHASE OPENED THE DOOR, his shotgun at the ready. He was surprised to find the sheriff's office empty. He had expected that Sheriff Moore, Judge Hathaway, maybe even Reese and Wade, would be there.

"I'll be damned," Chase said and then turned for the saloon. This time he kept the shotgun low so no one would panic. There were plenty of people drinking and playing cards, but he didn't see the men he sought. He set the gun on the bar, pointing toward Johnny. "You need to tell me where they are."

"Where who are?" Johnny asked, a sneer on his face.

"The Judge, sheriff and whoever else those two are with. I ain't gonna play nice anymore, so unless you want to eat lead, spill it."

The barkeep took one look at Chase, realized he meant what he said, and started spilling.

"They all went to Maggie's house. Something about getting what's owed the Judge. Said after he finishes with her he's coming for you. Said there's gonna be two trials at the same time. Yours and Maggie's."

Chase grimaced. He had to stop himself from pulling the trigger and killing Johnny. Instead he whirled around, leaving the barman breathing a sigh of relief. Chase left the saloon at a dead run.

CHAPTER TWENTY-NINE

Judge Hathaway was more than furious with Tom Moore. He wanted to tie him up and drag him behind his stagecoach for not keeping the drifter in custody.

"All you had to do, Tom, was to put that man in a cell and wait for me to return. When I tell you to do something, you do it. You don't think about it, you don't do something different, you do exactly as I say. Apparently, I made the wrong choice for sheriff. I should have made Jax sheriff. He does what he's told."

Sheriff Moore felt like pushing the Judge under the wheel of his stagecoach and rolling it over him. He was tired of taking orders from him. The small man strutted around everywhere he went, acting superior to all.

With great difficulty, the sheriff meekly said, "Yes, your honor, you're right. I messed up. It won't happen again, I can promise you that. You might want to ask Jax, who does what he's told, if he got you what you wanted from the Montgomery woman."

Hathaway glared at the sheriff, surprised at his insolence. He turned his attention to Jax, who had enjoyed seeing the sheriff get his ass chewed. The Judge waddled over to Jax, then stuck his hand out. "Give me what I wanted from that banker woman."

"Sorry, Judge, I don't have it. It's all Ed's fault, if you was to ask me," Jax said.

Judge Hathaway's face reddened and his hands shook as he sat down.

He looked around the room as he thought about his next move. Owen's daughter, Maggie, sat stiffly in a wooden chair. Sheriff Moore leaned against the wall, and Jax looked out the curtained window. The Judge knew he had to take possession of that homestead claim first, then find the I.O.U. to Owen.

"Sheriff, how dangerous is the drifter you let out? You think he will show up here?" Judge Hathaway asked.

"He's very dangerous. He's been accused of murder and also promised Maggie to find the real killer of her father. He'll come for you."

The Judge was skeptical. “Really? He’s that good? I have Reese and Wade outside and you and Jax in here. And we can use Miss Montgomery as a hostage if we have to.”

“We need more men. If you haven’t noticed, Jax has been shot in both hands. He can’t even hold a gun. We need Emmet. And what about Ed, Johnny and that old goat, Smiley?”

The Judge shook his head. “I’m not using Johnny for this. That would mean shutting down the saloon and losing a lot of money. Smiley is good at collecting debts, but he’s no gunfighter. I’m certain that Ed is drunk again, most likely passed out. That leaves Emmett. You really think having him here will tip this in our favor?”

“We need more guns, so yes, I do think that.”

The Judge glanced at Jax holding back the curtain with his bandaged hand and staring out the window. Making up his mind, he ordered, “Jax, go find Emmett and bring him here. And be quick about it.”

Jax let go of the window curtain and walked to the door. He fumbled with the doorknob, unable to turn it with his bandaged hands. “Damn it, someone open the door for me. I ain’t gonna find Emmet standing here.”

The sheriff opened the door for Jax. As he left, Jax

barked, "Don't kill that bastard before I get back. I wanna hurt him bad for what he done to me."

The Hanging Judge sat in Owen's office chair, thinking of how to persuade the woman to hand over the papers he needed. When he looked toward Maggie, she turned her head away, a defiant look on her pretty face. "Miss Montgomery, all this drama can stop right now if you just give me what I'm asking for. I know you have the papers, so give them to me before your new drifter friend gets killed. I give you my word that no harm will come to you if you cooperate."

Maggie didn't respond, hating every second the Judge sat in her father's chair. She felt that if she could stall a while Chase might come to find her. He said he would return, but she didn't know when. In the meantime, maybe she could do something to help Chase. "I have what you need, but first I need to know who killed my father."

Judge Hathaway leaned back in the chair and steepled his fingers over his ample stomach. "The man who met Owen on the outskirts of town killed him. I saw them together as I was traveling back to Split Rock. I gave his description to Emmett before I left for Dry Gulch, where I had to be for a trial the next day. He identified him at the saloon. Sheriff Moore arrested him, but somehow he got out. That's who killed your father."

Maggie knew the Judge was lying, because Chase told her he didn't do it and she believed him. "Well, Judge, I don't think you're being honest with me. I know that man did not kill my father."

"So, Miss Montgomery. You're calling me a liar then? I have no more time to waste on you and your ridiculous thoughts. As soon as this is over you will be tried for obstruction of justice in a murder case and slandering an elected official." Judge Hathaway turned to the sheriff. "Moore, tear this place apart and don't stop until you find me those papers. First, find something to tie this lying bitch up with. I don't want her getting away."

The sheriff felt sick as he took a length of cord from the window curtain and tied Maggie's hands behind her. He didn't like the way things were going and wanted to leave, but knew if he did Hathaway would have his hired guns kill him. So he started ripping the place to pieces, his anger growing with each minute. When he took a look at Maggie, he could swear she was smiling.

After the sheriff finished with the first floor, he went upstairs, to do the same.

Judge Hathaway remained at the large desk, opening each drawer and emptying the contents. Not able to find either paper, he stopped and took a look around the room. It was a complete shambles. The only place left to look was on Maggie. Maybe she'd hidden them under her clothes.

"Moore, get down here right now," he bellowed. The sheriff came slowly down the stairs, his clothes soaked with sweat, each step a struggle.

"What now?" he asked.

"Take her clothes off. She must be hiding the papers under them."

The sheriff was afraid of losing his job ... maybe even his life ... but he decided to draw the line. "I'm not gonna do that, Judge. I've done enough here tonight that I don't cotton to. If you want to search her that way, you do it. Get your own hands dirty for once."

"This will be the end of you, Moore."

"I don't give a damn. I ain't gonna strip her down, and that's final."

The sheriff sat down, still winded from his search of the house. He needed a drink in the worst way, so he poured himself one from the fancy decanter. He slugged it down, enjoying the warmth that spread through him.

He poured another, sipping it this time, as the Judge slithered over to Maggie.

CHAPTER THIRTY

Chase ran until he saw Maggie's house. The Judge's stagecoach was out front, so he kept to the shadows. Wade sat up top in the driver's seat, acting as a lookout. Every once in a while the coach bucked a little as the horses shifted their weight.

Reese stood at the corner of the house, the light from the window illuminating him. Chase changed his direction so that only Wade could see him as he got closer. He walked right up to the lead horses before Wade even saw him. Wade raised the coach gun, pointing it at Chase.

Before Wade could pull the trigger of the shotgun, Chase slapped the nearest horse, causing him to leap forward, which sent Wade tumbling to the ground. He never saw Chase's boot, which kicked him into blackness.

Reese heard the commotion and came out from behind the corner of the house, his pistol raised.

"Wade, what happened? What spooked the horses?" Reese reared back in surprise when, instead of seeing Wade as he'd expected, Chase appeared before him.

"Drop your piece. You don't have to die tonight," Chase said.

"I don't think that's an option for me, Mason. I work for the Judge, so I'll say the same to you. Drop the shotgun and I swear the Judge will not hang you."

"That's not likely."

"What's not likely? Dropping the shotgun or not hanging?"

"Both. Last chance, Reese. Do it now or I'll fill you full of lead."

Reese focused on Chase's eyes as he waited for the right moment to fire. They seemed to glow in the light from the windows as he swung the double barrel toward Reese. Flames billowed from both barrels as he pulled the trigger of his pistol.

The sound of the guns startled the horses and they lurched forward, trampling Wade. Reese lay on the cold ground, looking up at the moon, in the starless night. He couldn't feel any pain, but when he checked his body his hands fell into a hole where he felt what he assumed were his innards.

"I did warn you, Reese. You should have listened."

Reese was shocked. He was dying, No one opposed the Judge like this. Ever. He died then, the only light left in his eyes the moon's reflection.

Sheriff Moore knew that Chase was outside as soon as he heard the gun blast. He moved behind the desk and drew his gun. "You'd better get down, Judge, or you won't see tomorrow."

Judge Hathaway managed to drag Maggie, who was half dressed, behind the desk. "Woman, keep your mouth shut if you want to live. How many out there?" he asked the sheriff.

"Just one, I reckon. I'm sure it's the drifter, coming to save Maggie."

"He's not going to get her. I'll have you kill her first," the Judge said.

"I'm not killing her. You want her dead, shoot her yourself. You even have a gun?"

"Of course I have a gun," He showed Moore a fancy double-barreled derringer, shaking wildly in his fat hand. "If I have to, I will shoot her myself."

The front door burst open, followed by shotgun blasts. Chase entered the room, aiming at the walls.

Wood splinters flew everywhere. He reloaded the gun. Standing in the doorway as the dust settled, he yelled out, "Maggie, you all right?"

Before she could answer, the Judge pushed her in front of him, then stood behind her, his derringer pressed against the side of her head. "She's all right now, but won't be soon if you don't throw that gun down. This little gun I have will make a big hole in her if you don't do as I say."

Chase saw the derringer and the tears streaming down Maggie's face. He looked at the Judge. "You kill her like this you'll be hunted down for murder. Won't matter, you being a Judge and all."

"I won't be charged with murder. She has obstructed an official investigation and has been found guilty of such. It is in my authority to shoot her, but I am partial to hanging. Put down that shotgun if you want her to live."

Chase knew he could shoot the derringer out of the Judge's hand, but not with the shotgun. Maggie was standing too close. Chase slowly lowered the shotgun, squatting to put it on the floor. Now he felt confident he could put a bullet in the fat little man without hitting her.

"I'm guessing Tom Moore is there with you. Quit hiding and stand up, sheriff. Time to choose a side."

Sheriff Moore struggled to stand. His legs and back were stiff from kneeling behind the desk. He pointed his pistol at Chase.

"Mason, best you drop the gun belt. No one wants to see Maggie hurt. The Judge feels he has a legal right to end her life should he choose. Why not be a witness for her during the official trial? The courtroom is right outside, so both of you could be judged innocent in a few minutes if your testimony is compelling enough for the Judge."

"Really, Tom? You reckon that's even an option for us? We know what happens in that so-called courtroom."

Chase decided at that moment to shoot the sheriff with his left hand, then the Judge with his right. As he shifted his weight before drawing his guns, his head exploded with pain. His vision blurred as he collapsed to the floor.

CHAPTER THIRTY-ONE

Jax dropped the cast iron pan he'd hit Chase with and cradled his bandaged hands, which were now bleeding again, against his chest.

"WHAT TOOK YOU SO LONG?" the Judge screamed at Jax. "I could have been killed by that madman."

"SORRY, Judge. I looked all over town for Emmett. I didn't find him until I checked the saloon. Seems he was late paying, so Smiley was working him over real good with his knife. He ain't gonna be much help to you now."

. . .

"FORGET HIM. Sheriff, you take the drifter's guns and drag him into the courtroom." The Judge shoved Maggie toward Jax. "Jax, you take her and sit her next to him. Make sure their hands and feet are tied. Are Wade and Reese still outside? I'm gonna fire them right now for letting that man get in here."

Jax looked at the sheriff, then the Judge, and said, "Yep, they be outside, all right. But they ain't among the living no more. I dragged them to the back of the house, a little more out of sight."

"SAVES me the trouble of firing them. Jax, you can be my new driver. That should be no problem, even with those bandaged hands. Sheriff, I want you to turn in your badge tomorrow. You'll be my new hostler and ride shotgun. Now, let's get this trial underway.."

THE SHERIFF FELT like shooting Hathaway in the face, but he would be running from the law the rest of his life. He thought it better to go along with things now and then leave when the right time came.

JAX, on the other hand, was quite pleased with

himself, happy to be in good favor with Judge Hathaway, the most powerful man in the circuit.

THE JUDGE STRUGGLED to climb into the coach, his weight making the springs squeak as he entered. Sitting opposite the defendants, he wriggled his body to take maximum comfort from the cushioned seat.

MAGGIE GLARED AT HIM. "What kind of man does the things you do? How do you sleep at night?"

"NOW, now, Miss Montgomery. Let's keep this on the friendly side. Before court is in session, why not hand over the I.O.U. and claim. I'll drop all charges and you and your friend can go on with your lives."

CHASE GROANED. He slowly opened one eye, then the other. "What happened?" He tried to raise his hands to feel his head, then realized they were tied. Turning to Maggie he asked, "Are you hurt? Why are you half dressed?"

. . .

"I'M FINE, Chase. The Judge here thought I was hiding the paperwork he needs under my clothes."

CHASE HAD HEARD ENOUGH. "Let us go right now and I won't kill you."

THE JUDGE simply looked at him. "Enough foolish talk. If you won't give me the papers it's time to start the trial."

CHASE GLANCED AT MAGGIE. She shook her head no. He understood that she didn't want him to give the Judge what he carried under his shirt.

JUDGE HATHAWAY CLEARED HIS THROAT. "Welcome to the courtroom of the Honorable Judge Henry G. Hathaway. We are here to determine the guilt or innocence of the defendants. It is in your best interests to tell the complete truth. I am a fair man and will drop all charges against you should your testimony today warrant it. Please state your names for the court."

. . .

"THIS IS NONSENSE, PLAIN AND SIMPLE," Maggie said.

CHASE ADMIRED MAGGIE'S GUMPTION, but he needed time to think of a way out. "Let's go along with this for now. See what happens. We really don't have a choice."

THE JUDGE BANGED his gavel against the side of the carriage. "Quiet in the courtroom. One more outburst like that, I'll fine you for contempt. For the last time, state your names."

"MARGARET ANNE MONTGOMERY."

"CHASE MASON." As he said it, Chase noticed his father's name carved in the ceiling of the coach, just as Reese had told him.

. . .

THE JUDGE'S eyes widened when he heard the name, but didn't pursue it. He reached into his vest pocket, removing the tiny Bible that resided there. Holding it up, he asked, "Margaret Anne Montgomery, do you swear to tell the whole truth and nothing but the truth so help you God?"

"I DO."

HE TURNED TO CHASE. "Chase Mason, do you swear to tell the whole truth and nothing but the truth so help you God?"

"I DO."

"MISS MONTGOMERY, you have been charged with obstruction of an official investigation. How do you plead?"

"NOT GUILTY."

"Please state the reason for your plea."

. . .

"I DIDN'T DO ANYTHING. All I was trying to do, when you took me prisoner, was wait for Chase to come back."

"AND WHERE WAS Mr. Mason coming back from, Miss Montgomery?"

"A HORSEBACK RIDE."

"IS that all you have to say in your defense? Remember, you swore an oath to tell the whole truth." He tapped his vest pocket as he spoke.

MAGGIE HAD SWORN AN OATH, and she was an honest woman who followed the Scriptures on Sundays. If she didn't tell the truth under oath she would go against everything she believed in. "I don't have the I.O.U. or the homestead claim, but I know where they are."

. . .

"MAGGIE, don't. He'll kill us once he has what he wants," Chase said with conviction.

"MR. MASON. The court advises you to remain silent until you're called upon for your testimony. Miss Montgomery, please continue. You were saying you know where the documents are."

"YES, YOUR HONOR, I DO." Chase couldn't believe what he was hearing. Maggie was about to turn over the only things keeping them alive and there was no way to stop her. He held his gaze on Maggie, willing her to look at him. She didn't.

"BEFORE I REVEAL their location I need to know that the court will swear on that Bible to dismiss the charges against us and release us." Maggie looked the Judge in the eye, her gaze unwavering.

"YES, Miss Montgomery, of course. Upon hearing the location of the documents, and obtaining same, the court will drop the charges so you both will be free to go."

"WOULD you swear on that Bible you carry that what you say is true?" Maggie asked.

"YES, I swear on the Bible in my pocket that I speak the truth."

CHASE COULDN'T KEEP QUIET. "Maggie, don't tell him. Once he has them it's over for us. He can't be trusted."

MAGGIE TURNED her eyes from Chase as she said, "Thank you. They are in the bank, hidden, where no one but me will find them. Untie the ropes so we can go to the bank and get them for you."

"THANK YOU, Miss Montgomery. The court appreciates your honesty. However, the charges against you and Mr. Mason will not be dismissed. There will be no further testimony, as the court feels it has sufficient evidence to convict both of you." The Judge paused, letting the weight of his words hang in the air. "For the charge of obstruction of an official investigation, the court hereby finds the defendant, Margaret Anne Montgomery, guilty as charged. The punishment for this crime shall be death by hanging, to be carried out immediately following this trial. For the charge of the murder of Owen James Montgomery, the court hereby finds the defendant, Chase Mason, guilty as charged. The punishment for this crime shall be death by hanging, to be carried out as soon as possible."

"I DON'T UNDERSTAND. You swore on your Bible that we would be released!" Maggie yelled.

JUDGE HATHAWAY REACHED BACK into his vest pocket and laughed as he removed the small book.

"IT'S NOT EVEN a real Bible. It just looks like one." He fanned the tiny pages, showing her that each was blank.

. . .

"I SUSPECT your faith is what convinced you to tell the truth. Look at it this way: If you decided not to tell me, you would be hanging right now." He let that sink in for a moment, then said, "While I'm at the bank, getting what's mine, I suggest you make your peace. I'll be back before you know it."

MAGGIE'S delicate hands clenched into fists. "You lying skunk. You should be ashamed of yourself. The Devil has a special place for people like you."

THE JUDGE MADE his way through the carriage door, looking back before stepping down. "Too bad for you I don't believe in the Devil. Sheriff, help me down. We'll come back to hang these two later."

CHAPTER THIRTY-TWO

Before he exited the courtroom, Judge Hathaway pulled the window shades. As he stepped down, his considerable weight shook the coach enough to open the shades just enough to see out.

"You'll pay for this one way or another," Chase hissed as he glared out the small slit in the shades. Maggie and Chase watched silently as the hanging Judge and his cronies made their way to the bank and kicked the door open.

Chase wriggled both hands, trying to loosen his bonds. "Why did you say the papers were at the bank when you know I have them?"

Maggie's eyes glistened with tears. "I didn't know what else to do. We have no one to help us out of this.

I was trying to get us more time, maybe even convince the Judge to bring us to the bank. I thought if he did maybe you could overpower them."

Maggie's tears broke Chase's heart. What kind of gunslinger was he that he couldn't even protect her? She looked so helpless, sitting beside him, half dressed. All he could do now was give her some hope, so he said, "That was quick thinking. At least we're still alive, so there's a chance we could get out of this. Maybe someone will see us in here if we start yelling."

He sucked in a deep breath and was about to yell for help when the stagecoach started moving. Chase and Maggie exchanged surprised glances.

"I didn't see anyone leave the bank, so who's driving," Chase asked. He looked to Maggie. "Whatever happens next, be ready. When we stop, if they get close to the door, I'll try to knock them over. It's the only play we have."

Maggie looked skeptical. "But your hands are tied."

"Maybe the rope will break when I hit the ground. Or maybe I'll fall on top of him and choke the life out of him. I don't know how it's gonna play out, Maggie. All I know is that I plan to fight until my last breath to protect you."

Maggie stared at Chase, feelings for him welling up

inside her. She couldn't believe this was the man she thought killed her father. "Thank you, Chase."

She had to look away. Maggie couldn't bear the thought of not having the chance to repay him for his help and kindness. Both remained silent, sitting together but thinking separate thoughts, as the stagecoach made its way along. After a few minutes, the coach came to a sudden stop, rocking a few times before settling to stillness.

They heard the driver climbing down, then footsteps shuffling toward the door. Chase tensed every muscle in his lean body, ready to pounce as soon as the door opened. Maggie felt his body change and saw the look of determination on his face. She closed her eyes, praying for a miracle. Chase watched intently as the handle turned quickly and the door started to open. He launched his body just as he heard, "Mr. Mason, I have Rebel."

The door opened violently, knocking the stable boy off his feet. Chase rolled when he hit the ground. Ben was still down, dazed by the force of the door hitting him. Chase struggled to his feet, stumbling to Ben.

"Hey, kid. I didn't know it was you. Get up. We don't have much time before they figure things out."

Ben sat up slowly, the dizziness fading.

"How did you know we were in the stagecoach?" Chase turned around and held his bound hands up. Ben took out his pocketknife and started sawing away at the rope.

"I followed you to the saloon. Figured there would be trouble and I wanted to make things right with you. I watched you take care of those hired men at Maggie's house, then I waited. I saw them leave you in the stagecoach, so I stole it. Am I in some big trouble now?"

"Not with me, kid. Just finish cutting me loose, then help Maggie get out." Chase pointed to the driver's seat. "Is that my rifle?"

'Yes sir. I kinda borrowed it from Rebel. He didn't seem to mind."

Chase took the rope that Ben had cut from his hands and feet, draping it loosely around his neck. "I need to stop those men. Stay here and keep Maggie safe." He handed Ben one of his pistols and climbed into the driver's seat.

"If I don't come back, get on Rebel with Maggie and ride west until you come to a town called Amberton. Go to the Golden Goose Saloon and ask for Maria. Tell her I sent you. You'll be safe there."

"But, what if……" Chase left before Ben could finish his question, the coach slowly making its way back toward Main Street. He parked it exactly where it had been before and set the handbrake. He took his rifle and climbed back in, this time sitting in the comfortable padded seat.

Chase propped the Winchester .44-40 against the door on the opposite side of where he sat. It wasn't much longer before he spotted the trio coming out of the bank. It seemed like forever before they got close to the stagecoach.

Chase heard Hathaway tell the Sheriff and Jax to bury the bodies of Reese and Wade. He didn't want any locals to find them and cause a ruckus. Jax removed a shovel from the back of the coach and both men disappeared.

The door opened and the Judge poked his head in. He hesitated, clearly surprised that the bench was empty. Then he turned his head in Chase's direction.

A viselike grip pulled him the rest of the way in. Chase threw him on the wooden seat, then lashed his hands together. The Judge was so startled all he could do was wheeze and blow bubbles out his nose. Chase punched him in the face, knocking him out so he wouldn't call out to the others. He climbed up to the driver's seat, released the brake and quietly commanded the team to go. Chase was counting on both men digging graves out back to be too busy to notice any noise the stage made.

He drove the stagecoach the back way to the stable, parking it where Ben had earlier. He jumped down and silently entered the dimly lit barn.

Maggie stood by Rebel's stall, feeding him a handful of oats, while Ben polished the pistol Chase had handed him. When he cleared his throat, both Maggie and Ben jumped at the sound.

Maggie spilled the rest of the oats in the dirt and ran to him. Her arms went around his waist and she hugged him with all her strength. He laughed and lifted her high over his head with ease. He put her down, stroking her hair and running his fingers along her cheek. Her skin was as smooth as the well-worn wooden grips of his pistols.

He smiled down at her. "Wait 'til you see the surprise I brought you."

He told Ben to stay and watch for the sheriff and Jax.

"What if I see them? What am I gonna do?"

"Give a whistle, kid. You know how?"

"Course I can whistle. Wanna hear?"

"Later, Ben. I have some things to take care of. Keep an eye out. I'm counting on you."

Chase wheeled, taking Maggie along with him.

When she saw the stagecoach she tried to stop, but Chase picked her up in his arms, carrying her to the door. He gently let her down and opened the door. She looked in to see the Judge sitting up, blood on his face. "Please get in Maggie. He can't hurt you now."

Maggie climbed into the stagecoach, entering the courtroom slowly. Chase followed her and they sat together on the cushioned seat. He leaned over and took the tiny Bible from the Judge's vest pocket.

Chase cleared his throat, held up the book and said, "Welcome to the courtroom of the Honorable Judge Henry G. Hathaway. We are here to determine the guilt or innocence of the defendant. It is in your best interests to tell the complete truth. This is a fair court that will drop all charges against you should your testimony here today warrant it. Henry G. Hathaway, do you swear to tell the whole truth and nothing but the truth, so help you God?"

"What is the meaning of this? I am the Honorable Judge Henry G. Hathaway. Release me immediately or I will … ."

"You will what?" Chase interrupted. "You already sentenced us to hang. What more can you do?"

"Well, I might be able to convince the court to dismiss all pending charges. You would have to release me right now, though."

"Your honor, that is a very generous offer, to be sure. But not enough to free you. Do you have anything else you could add to the pot? Anything at all?"

"I have no other offerings at this time."

"All right then. The court has heard your testimony and will now take a few moments to decide your fate."

Chase took a cartridge from his pocket, placed it between his thumb and forefinger, and made it dance its way across his fingers. He did this a few times while Maggie and the Judge watched in fascination. The cartridge came to a sudden stop and Chase put it away. "The court has reached a verdict."

Chase glanced at Maggie as he spoke the sentence. "Henry G. Hathaway, this court has found you guilty of all charges. You are hereby sentenced to hang until all life is gone from your body. We will ask the hangman to let you sway a little extra, due to your disservice to all those innocent souls you condemned. The hanging is to be right here, right now. If you have any last words, we advise you to speak them, or bring them with you to Hell."

Chase didn't say another word, but left the courtroom, returning with the hanging rope from the back of the stagecoach. He managed to push up enough on the ceiling to loop the rope over the oak framework.

He slid it along the beam until it was directly over the Judge. Handing the end of the rope to Maggie, he admired the noose before placing it around the Judge's neck.

"What in God's name do you think you're doing? Get that dirty rope off me. It was used just days ago to hang someone for attempted murder of an elected official." Sweat drenched his face and collar, and he had a wild look in his eyes.

"Reese, Wade, help me," he screamed, spittle flying. He was so frightened he forgot they were dead. Chase snugged the noose a little tighter, then sat next to Maggie. Taking the loose end of the rope from her, he pulled on it until there was no slack left. He tied it to an iron ring on the floor of the coach.

The Judge squirmed and then blurted out, "Wait, wait! I could give you ten-thousand dollars. I think that would suffice, don't you agree?"

"The court will take it under consideration. We do, however, have a few more questions before we allow you an appeal."

"Yes, please ask. I'll answer anything."

"Judge Hathaway, do you know who killed Owen James Montgomery?"

"Yes, but if you could take this filthy noose from my neck I would be able to talk easier. Do you swear to drop the charge of murder and all other charges if I tell you what I know?"

"Yes, of course. This court will drop all charges as long as you tell the truth -- the whole truth. For the last time, who killed Owen James Montgomery?"

Maggie leaned forward in anticipation of his answer, but none came. Chase tightened the rope. The Judge shouted out, "I killed him. It was me. I mean to say, I paid someone to kill him for me."

"Please tell the court why you wanted him dead."

"I borrowed ten-thousand dollars from him and he kept it off the books. No one else knew, not even his daughter. I wanted to keep it for myself."

"Please tell the court why you needed the money."

"Enough of this foolishness! Take this rope off me right now. This is not a courtroom and you are not a judge. I'm not saying another word without my solicitor present."

He glowered at Chase and Maggie defiantly.

"I demand you send for him. His name is Jacob Wellerhorn. He lives over in Rivertown, just about five days' ride from here. You can put me in jail until he arrives to represent me."

"The court has found you in contempt. I believe that's about an extra ten minutes viewing time for the people of Split Rock. I'm certain they will enjoy seeing you hang from your own rope."

Chase jerked the rope tight, causing the Judge to panic again.

"All right! Sweet Jesus, I beg you, stop pulling the rope."

Chase released some pressure on the rope so Hathaway could breathe and talk easier.

"I was enjoying a drink or two with Owen one evening. Apparently, he doesn't drink often, because after only two shots he told me that Chester Hale made him the beneficiary of his estate. Did it all up legal, even drew up a will. Then I happened to hear that Chester had a homestead claim for five-hundred acres. Includes a mountain and a creek. Those are good places to find gold, so I thought up a plan. Like I said, I got the ten-thousand, and then I convinced old Chester to name me as beneficiary, instead of Owen. He didn't want to do it, so I had my men rough him up a bit. Eventually, he decided to change it. Chester was killed by some drifter who was caught and sentenced to hang by my court. We took care of the hanging quickly, to show respect for Mr. Hale. It was the least we could do."

"Did that drifter have Chester's ten-thousand on him when he was caught?"

"He didn't. We searched Hale's place top to bottom and it wasn't there. That drifter must have buried it or hid it somewhere. None of this so-called testimony matters anyway. You have no proof I borrowed the money from Owen and there is no claim to substantiate the story I just told."

"Well, you're right about one thing. We don't have the ten-thousand you borrowed from Owen.

But we believe you know where it is."

"All this means nothing. Obviously you don't have the paperwork, because the bank is all torn up, just like Owen's house. Without that, without the money, you would be hanging a man with no real proof. A judge, no less. Every lawman in the country would be hunting you for the reward. Speaking of lawmen, was your father Ned Mason, a Pinkerton?"

"What's it matter to you?"

"Means nothing that he was your father. I keep track of all lawmen killed in the field. Just means a bonus for me if I catch and hang the murderer is all. Will you release me now that I told you what I know?"

"Just a few more loose ends to clean up. You owed that money to Owen. With him dead, you need to pay it back to Maggie. This is your last chance to do the right thing."

"I have no idea where the money is. My apologies."

Chase heaved on the rope, lifting the portly man partially off the seat. Judge Hathaway flailed his bound arms wildly, his jowled face turning dark red, then purple. He tried to say something but it was garbled, and his bloodshot eyes bulged. Before he stopped breathing, Chase lowered him back to the bench seat and loosened the noose.

Chase gave him a moment, then reached inside his shirt. "Take a look here, Hathaway."

He showed the Judge the I.O.U. and the homestead claim.

Once Hathaway saw the documents, he knew it was over. His voice raspy, the Judge immediately told them everything. He had the money. He'd never paid Chester, even though Chester did change the will. The Judge decided to have him killed and hired a drifter to do it. Then he declared the drifter guilty and had him hanged to cover his tracks. He was going to do the same to Chase.

"The money is inside the cushion you are sitting on. It's all there, you don't have to count it."

Maggie felt as though she was moving in thick mud. It sickened her that her father was murdered for ten-thousand dollars by a man he thought of as a friend.

Not to mention poor Mister Hale. A gentle man living a quiet life just trying to do the right thing.

"Chase, get me out of here. I can't breathe."

Chase opened the door, lifted Maggie to her feet and carried her down the step. They left the Judge in the stagecoach, the rope still around his neck.

CHAPTER THIRTY-THREE

Maggie wobbled into the barn, desperate for some water to splash on her face. She stopped in her tracks when she heard Ben franticly trying to whistle. The only sound coming out was a blowing noise. Maggie ran as fast as she could back outside to warn Chase. He lifted her effortlessly, carrying her back into the barn. He put her in Rebel's stall. "You'll be safe here. Stay here until I come get you."

All she could manage was a nod. Chase walked quickly away, ready to do anything to protect her. He told Ben to stay quiet as he readied his pistol, then got behind one of the large wooden beams that supported the old barn. He suspected it would be the sheriff coming to help the Judge, and he might have some others with him.

"Ben, throw down the pistol I gave you. Try to have it land on a bale of hay."

The pistol seemed to fall in slow motion. It hit a wooden peg, bounced off, then hit the top rail of a stall, landing on the edge of a bale only a few feet from Chase. He darted out to grab it, then returned to his hiding spot. He heard voices where the stagecoach was parked. No doubt the Judge had sent someone to kill them. The small door on the side of the barn flew open, snapping right off its hinges. Emmett Blackman ran in holding a shotgun.

"Shoot him, Emmett. He tried to kill the Judge," the sheriff screamed.

Emmett fired both barrels without ever seeing Chase. The smoke from the blast filled the barn and Chase heard the shotgun being reloaded. He didn't want to kill Emmett, so he stepped out and shot him once in the leg. Emmett went down screaming,

"He shot me, he shot me! Help, I'm bleeding bad." The sheriff rushed into the smoke-filled barn, gun drawn and ready to fire. He couldn't see much and tripped. He panicked and backed up to a post, wondering where Chase was.

"Well, Tom, you can either drop the handgun or die. Your choice," Chase's voice floated out of the darkness.

Chase was to his left, but hard to place. He fired two shots toward where he thought Chase was hiding. He heard one bullet hit something, then a muffled grunt. The sheriff yelled out, "I got him, Emmett. I just shot Mason."

He ran toward where he'd heard the bullet hit. He reached down to roll the drifter's body over, but when he did he gasped. He'd shot Emmett.

Emmett was dead, his hand with a missing finger still clutching the shotgun. The sheriff crouched, trying to make himself as small a target as possible. He wished he'd never met the Judge or heard of Split Rock. He couldn't wait to start a new life with the money the Judge had promised him. He remained crouching until his leg muscles burned. When he couldn't take the pain any longer, he stood up slowly. He stared into the smoke, looking for any kind of movement. He saw nothing, but heard that hollow voice again.

"Looks like you made your choice, Moore. Don't say I didn't warn you."

The Sheriff panicked and fired all his remaining

shots toward the voice. He heard wood splintering, and one of them must have hit something solid as a ricochet buzzed by him like an angry bee. He bent a knee to reload, his shaking fingers unable to place the cartridges into the chambers quickly. He managed to get two cartridges in before he felt the cold steel of a gun barrel pressed against his head.

"Last chance, Tom. Put the gun down now and live. You'll spend the rest of your life in jail, but you'll be alive."

"I don't like the sound of that, Mason."

The sheriff turned as quickly as he could, but couldn't get a shot off before Chase's gun roared right beside his head, blowing out his eardrum. Chase followed up with a punch, knocking the sheriff out cold.

Chase stood, listening and waiting for the next attacker to come through the door.

The gun blasts terrified Maggie. Bullets and splinters of wood flew everywhere. Worst of all, she heard someone say they'd just shot Chase. As the smoke started to clear, Maggie struggled to her feet, forcing herself to go to the front of the stall. If she was going to die, she wanted to be standing, even if she was afraid.

When no one else came in shooting, Chase made his way slowly to Rebel's stall. He didn't want to scare Maggie or the horse. As he drew closer, he saw Maggie, then Rebel, their heads leaning over the railing. Both stared intently in his direction. Rebel whinnied and Maggie yelled out at the same time, a sound Chase would take to the grave. He ran to them, hugging first one, then the other.

"Let's get out of here. I need some fresh air." Chase yelled up to the loft. "Hey, Ben, come on down. It's over."

The boy made his way down the ladder, trying to hide the tears of joy streaking down his face He had feared the drifter would not make it out alive. He hugged Maggie, then Rebel, and finally, Chase.

Chase opened the stall door, and removed the saddle, saddle blanket and bridle. He put Rebel's halter on, then walked the horse to the corral. The horse ran around the fenced-in area like a young colt, which brought a smile to Chase's face. Turning to Maggie, he asked her to take Ben home. "I have some unfinished business here. Sheriff Moore needs the doc to look him over and the Judge needs to be locked in a jail cell until the marshals get here. I'll see you both tomorrow."

Maggie held Ben's hand, as they walked toward his home.

Chase went in the stable and stood over the sheriff, who was just coming around. "Why didn't you kill me, Mason? I wanted you to," the sheriff said.

"I don't like killing people. You should know that already. I shot you in the arm and Jax in each hand. By the way, where was Jax when you tried to kill me?"

"Drinking at the saloon. He has to hold his glass with both hands. No way he could hold a gun, let alone fire one."

"Me shooting his hands has changed him for the better. You know you killed Emmett, right? You'll be tried for murder for that."

"I know, but it was an accident. I never should have fired with all that gun smoke."

"You could have been one of the good ones, Moore." Chase reached down and plucked the badge from Tom Moore's shirt. "You didn't deserve to wear this. It will be easy for the people of Split Rock to find someone better than you."

The doctor arrived with a buckboard, taking Tom Moore to his office and Emmett to the undertaker. Chase went out to the stagecoach, intending to drive it to the sheriff's office. He wanted to park it there and let the Judge see it from his cell. He looked in and stopped short. He climbed in and sat opposite the man. There he was, in his fine clothes and polished boots, slowly swaying from his own rope, the once mighty and feared Hanging Judge of Split Rock.

CHAPTER THIRTY-FOUR

Chase got out of the tub of steaming water after scrubbing himself for what seemed like hours. His long dark hair was now clean and his face shaven. He glanced at his bed where he had slept soundly for twelve hours despite the fact that it was too small for him.

His laundered clothes were folded on the nearby dresser, silently reminding him to get a move on. This morning, Maggie's lawyer would advise her if she was the legal owner of Chester's claim. Chase didn't know much about the law, but he did know when someone was trying to pull a fast one.

He dressed quickly, then pulled his highly polished boots on, suddenly feeling as if he was heading to a funeral. He didn't know who had arranged for all the cleaning, but they should not have made his boots look so good. He scuffed them up so he didn't look like a dandy.

Chase strapped on his guns, checking to make sure each was loaded and ready to fire. He grabbed his black hat from the wall hook and shut the door behind him, heading for the bank to protect Maggie.

MAGGIE WOKE SLOWLY, not wanting to leave the comfort of her bed. Sunlight filtered in through the shades and rippled glass of the windows as she thought about the recent changes in her life.

The murder of her father would affect her for the rest of her days, but she was pleased she'd had a hand in finding his killer. Maggie owed a debt of gratitude to Chase Mason for his help in the matter. She was determined to pay him back, regardless of how long it might take. She smiled as she thought about him. He was so damn good looking, with that black hair and those blue eyes. So tall and strong, with a willingness to help others even when he had his own troubles.

She sighed and then threw back the blanket. Her father's lawyer, Eugene Talbot, was scheduled to meet her at the bank to wade through the tangle of legal matters. She soaked in the tub until the water started to cool, then dressed in her finest dress. Maggie wanted to look her best for Chase. After a last long look in the mirror, she adjusted her dress slightly, grabbed her handbag and headed for the bank. She didn't know if she was more excited to hear the legal news or to see Chase.

At the bank, Maggie sat at her father's desk examining bank statements. She was so involved with the paperwork that when the door opened it startled her. She looked up to see her father's lawyer holding a briefcase in one hand and his derby in the other.

"Good morning, Miss Montgomery. May we get started right away? I have several other pressing legal matters to attend to as soon as this meeting concludes."

"I'm sorry, Mr. Talbot, but we must wait for my friend to arrive before we can begin. I hope you don't mind."

Eugene glanced at his pocket watch. "Of course not, as long as your friend arrives promptly. I have approximately five extra minutes to spare."

"I'm sure he'll be here shortly. So sorry to inconvenience you. Perhaps you should have mentioned your time constraints when we arranged this meeting,"

Maggie said, smiling sweetly to counteract the sting in her words.

He hung his derby on the hat tree and started pacing the office. “Do you mind if I smoke a cigar while we wait?”

“Yes, I mind. I would appreciate it if you don’t light that disgusting thing. I’m wearing my best dress and I don’t want it smelling like a rotting carcass.”

The lawyer glared at her, looked longingly at the cigar, then put it back in his pocket. “Your father didn’t mind if I smoked.”

Before Maggie could reply, Chase opened the door and stepped briskly into the bank. He looked directly at the lawyer.

“I hope I’m not in the way here, but I want to make sure Maggie isn’t taken advantage of.” He offered his hand to the lawyer, “I’m Chase Mason, a close friend.”

The lawyer shook Chase’s hand. “Eugene Talbot, Owen’s lawyer. Maggie contacted me and asked if I would look into several legal matters for her.”

Maggie stared at Chase, hardly believing this was the same man she’d met just days ago. Clean-shaven and dressed in clean clothes, he was without a doubt, the most handsome man she’d ever laid eyes on. All she wanted to do was put her arms around him and kiss him. Barely able to restrain herself, she told Chase to take a seat.

"Mr. Talbot, we're ready to hear your findings."

"Right, then. Let's get started." Talbot placed his briefcase on Owen's desk, opened it and removed several papers. "I assume you have Owen's will in your possession?"

"I have it. It seems pretty straightforward to me. Everything he owned is now mine. Right?" Maggie asked.

Chase could tell that this was the moment. He leaned forward, staring intently at the man as he waited to hear his reply.

The lawyer shuffled some papers, read one of them. "Yes, Miss Montgomery. That is correct." He slipped the papers back into the briefcase and closed it. "I've examined the land claim at length along with Chester's will. There is nothing wrong with the land claim; it's a legal document. However, the will showed Owen's name crossed out and Henry Hathaway's name written in. Legally, Hathaway becomes the owner of the claim, even if Mr. Hale was forced to change it."

Chase asked, "How is that possible? We know he was forced to do it. He wanted Owen in his will, not Hathaway."

"Doesn't matter. The law is the law." The lawyer paused to look at Maggie. "With the death of Henry Hathaway, I had to examine his will to see who he named beneficiary."

Maggie's stomach fluttered, "Who is named?"

"Tom Moore. He now owns everything the Judge had, including the land claim."

"But what about the I.O.U. I showed you? That must mean something."

"It means nothing unless you can prove that the money Mr. Hathaway borrowed from Owen was never given to Chester Hale. If I send a marshal over there and he finds the cash, then Mr. Moore owns the claim."

Chase stood in front of the lawyer and looked down at him. "If you come with me I can prove that Chester Hale either never received the money or Hathaway stole it back from him when he had him killed. I know right where the Judge hid it."

Maggie, Chase and the lawyer left the bank, heading for the stable. The trio walked purposely to the stagecoach parked inside. Chase opened the door and climbed in, motioning for the lawyer to follow. "Sit there," he told the man, as he pointed to the very seat the Judge had occupied before hanging himself.

Maggie hesitated. "Chase, I don't think I can go in there again. I feel faint just being this close."

"You don't have to, Maggie. I just need to show Mr. Talbot where Hathaway hid the cash."

Chase kneeled down next to the padded seat and tore it open with his hands. He reached in, his fingers searching for the money. He finally stood up, wads of bills clutched in his hands. "It was right where Hathaway said it was. Will that be enough proof for you?"

Talbot looked at the money. "You and Miss Montgomery will have to sign a sworn statement, stating what the Judge confessed. I'll have to run it by the magistrate, but I believe that will be sufficient."

"We will do that. This money belongs to Maggie, so I reckon we can take it now."

"Yes, it does. But you can't take possession of it just yet. There is a tremendous amount of legal work I have to complete first. It will be very expensive, but in the end, Maggie will receive all that she is entitled to. Minus my fee of course."

"Any idea how long that will take?" Chase asked.

"This is a complicated legal matter. Everything must be documented and approved. It could take several months to complete the paperwork. You'll have to be patient. Rest assured, Mr. Mason, I will do my best to expedite the proceedings. This matter is of utmost importance and I will give it my undivided attention."

Chase gathered all the cash, stacked it as best he could, and showed it to Maggie. "It's all yours, but you'll have to hand it over to Mr. Talbot until the paperwork is done."

Maggie watched as her lawyer scooped the money into his briefcase. "I trust you, Eugene, because my father did. I just need to document the transfer of cash so I have a record of it."

"Of course, Miss Montgomery, of course. I'll write a signed receipt as soon as I get back to my office. You'll have it by the end of the day." He climbed out of the stagecoach, tipped his hat and left.

"Thank God that money was there, Chase. If the Judge had lied about that, things would stand a lot different right now," Maggie said.

"That's a fact, Maggie, but I knew he wasn't lying. I will say that we should have taken it the day he died, but there were too many other things happening. To be honest, I kind of forgot about it. Turned out to be a good thing, because we were able to prove to Talbot that it was hidden here."

Chase looked at Maggie in her fancy dress. He wanted to pick her up and kiss her. He couldn't explain why he felt so awkward around her. He thought she wanted him to kiss. "Your skin looks as soft as Rebel's muzzle," he said.

Maggie laughed out loud as she turned to him. "You really know how to compliment a girl. I have never had a man tell me that before." She reached up and pulled him closer. Standing on her toes, she kissed him before he could pull back. She loved the way he kissed her back, then held her tightly, stroking her cheek with the back of his hand. "Well, who has softer skin, me or Rebel?"

Chase chuckled and said, "I don't think I should answer that. I will tell you that you kiss better than he does."

They both laughed. Holding hands, they walked back to the bank.

CHASE STAYED in town until Maggie received all the legal documents naming her the rightful owner of the Hale claim, the ten-thousand dollars and her father's estate.

Before leaving, he explained why he couldn't stay even though he wanted to. He needed to go to Long Pine and follow up on the leads he'd gathered while in Split Rock. He promised to visit her when he could.

Maggie didn't cry in front of Chase the day he left. She hid that for later.

Chase stopped by the stable on his way out of town, to thank Ben and say goodbye. Ben was outside, standing beside a saddled horse and a mule with a huge pack lashed to its back.

"What's in the pack?" Chase asked.

"Everything we need for traveling. Food for the horses and my mule, canned goods and coffee, water and … ."

"Whoa, stop right there. What do you mean, 'for traveling?' I didn't ask you to join me."

"I know, but I asked my Ma and she agreed that I could go. So all you have to do is say yes. I'll take care of the animals, make camp, do all the chores and anything else needs doing. I won't even ask for a wage if that's what you're worried about."

Chase looked at the boy. He might be helpful along the trail, but he didn't want to have to look after someone.

Ben stared at him expectantly, a pleading look in his eyes. "Please, Mr. Mason. I'll be no trouble. I promise you won't regret it. If you say no, I'm gonna follow you anyway."

Chase sighed. The kid had that determined look in his eye and he supposed it would be better to have the boy in camp rather than outside on his own. "Kid, did I ever tell you why I came to Split Rock?"

"No, sir, you didn't."

"Saddle up. I'll tell you after we stop at your Ma's place. I want to make sure she knows what we'll be facing along the way. She might change her mind about you coming along."

"She won't. You might as well start telling me the story."

Chase smiled to himself as he gave Rebel a nudge with his knees. The horse bucked a little before settling into a canter.

****

SIGNUP for my newsletter and be the first to know when the next Chase Mason adventure is released:

https://bruceeverett.gr8.com

ABOUT THE AUTHOR

Bruce Everett is a lover of Western stories from way back. A former stall mucker, computer technician and airplane handler, Bruce lives in New Hampshire with his wife and his dog and spends his days fishing Lake Winnepesaukee and nights writing about the old west.

Signup for email alerts for his next release in the Chase Mason Gunslinger series here:
https://bruceeverett.gr8.com

Follow Bruce on Amazon here:
http://amazon.com/author/bruceeverettauthor

This is a work of fiction.

None of it is real. All names, places, and events are products of the author's imagination. Any resemblance to real names, places, or events are purely coincidental, and should not be construed as being real.

THE HANGING JUDGE OF SPLIT ROCK

❀ Created with Vellum

Made in the USA
Columbia, SC
11 December 2019